HRJC

C0-DXC-202

JURASSIK DIARIES

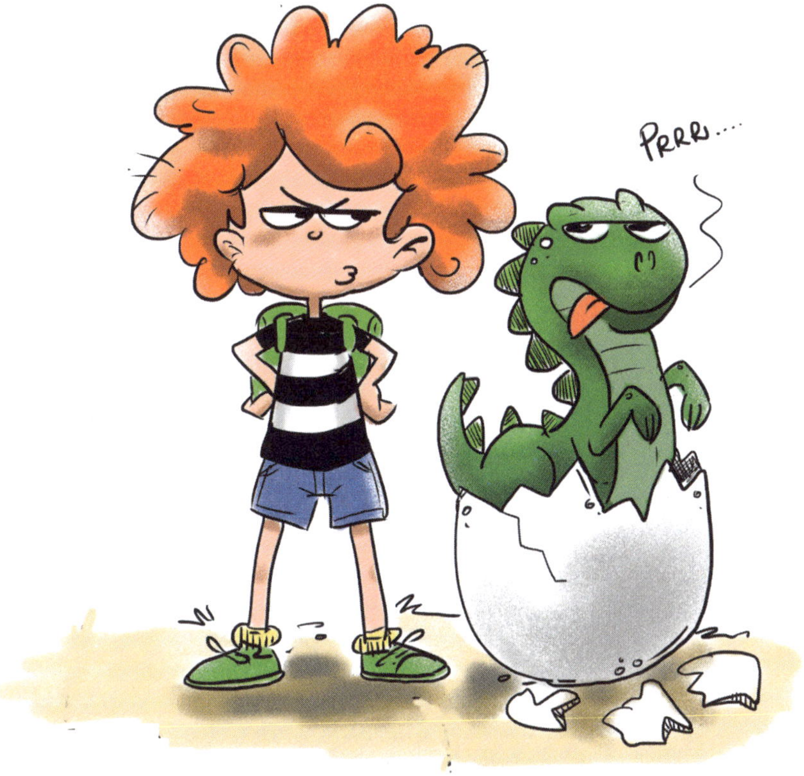
PRRR....

ABLAZE

Almond Project presents

JURASSIK DIARIES

Copyright © Philip Osbourne
Illustrations: Roberta Procacci

Editing: Ilaria Belletti
Literary Agent: Plume Studio

FOR ABLAZE
Managing Editor
Rich Young
Editor
Kevin Ketner
Designer
Rodolfo Muraguchi

Publisher's Cataloging-in-Publication data

Names: Osbourne, Philip, author.
Title: Jurassik diaries , volume 1 / Philip Osbourne.
Description: Portland, OR: Ablaze Publishing, 2022.
Identifiers: ISBN: 978-1-950912-46-9
Subjects: LCSH Dinosaurs— Comic books, strips, etc. | Time travel— Comic books, strips, etc. | Science fiction—Comic books, strips, etc. | Graphic novels. | BISAC JUVENILE FICTION / Comics & Graphic Novels / Humorous | JUVENILE FICTION / Historical / Prehistory
Classification: LCC PZ7.1.O82 Jur vol. 1 2022 | DDC 741.5—dc23

JURASSIK DIARIES. Published by Ablaze Publishing, 11222 SE Main St. #22906 Portland, OR 97269. Jurassik Diaries © 2020 Philip Osbourne. All Rights Reserved. Ablaze and its logo TM & © 2022 Ablaze, LLC. All Rights Reserved. All names, characters, events, and locales in this publication are entirely fictional. Any resemblance to actual persons (living or dead), events or places, without satiric intent is coincidental. No portion of this book may be reproduced by any means (digital or print) without the written permission of Ablaze Publishing except for review purposes. Printed in Mexico. This book may be purchased for educational, business, or promotional use in bulk. For sales information, advertising opportunities and licensing email: info@ablazepublishing.com

10 9 8 7 6 5 4 3 2 1

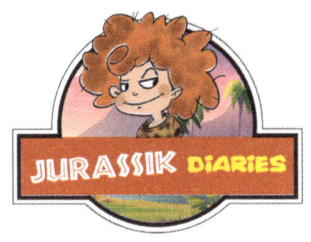

PHILIP OSBOURNE

JURASSIK DIARIES

Illustrations by Roberta Procacci

A NEW WORLD

CHAPTER ONE
Back to school!

Dear Diary,
Do you know why the Tyrannosaur class has no teachers?
Of course! Tyrannosaurs have a bad habit of eating them!

HAVE A GUESS:
DO T-REX TEACHERS ALWAYS FORGET THEIR COATS OR DO THE T-REXES DEVOUR THEM BEFORE THE END OF THE LESSON?

I'm not joking!
When I arrived here, I asked around in Jurassika what the Tyrannosaurus were doing.

JURASSIK DIARIES

The stegosaurs, who really can't stand them, told me that almost all of them are scavengers.
I had a good laugh!
Scavengers!
Ah! Ah! Ah! Ah! Ah! Ah! Ah! Ah! Ah!

Are the terrible tyrannosaurs, the top of the food chain, cute garbage collectors?
Unfortunately, I didn't quite understand: Tyrannosaurs are "strange scavengers"... they devour everything that comes their way... including.teachers!

CHAPTER ONE

That's why I immediately took a job as a teacher. The other dinosaurs say that the Tyrannosaur is a mouth that walks on two legs... and I think there is some truth to it. They are intelligent animals, but they don't understand the silliest of rules: "Don't eat others!"

DON'T EAT OTHERS!

JURASSIK DIARIES

You should know that only one thing, and one thing only, makes them nice and smiley...
Are you curious to know what it is?
T-Rexes are nice if you blow raspberries at them... and they'll laugh their heads off if you dress like a clown.

Don't ask me why... but if you want to see the teeth of a T-Rex without having to go down its throat, you'd better learn how to blow raspberries!

CHAPTER ONE

Now you know why they won't eat me... they wait until the end of class to hear one of my super raspberries.
In fact, before they get impatient:

PRRRRR!!!!

After my raspberry, I can teach them a bit of science... and history... and make them understand what will happen to them if they don't listen to me. They don't know everything I do because, if you haven't noticed, besides being handsome and fascinating, I am a genius who has studied a lot... and I know that the ice age will come soon. Yes, here in Jurassika, everything will soon freeze, and they will become extinct. However, now I'm here, and I will save them!

They will become extinct!

NOW I WILL ILLUSTRATE WHAT WILL **HAPPEN** TO EACH ONE OF YOU IF YOU DECIDE NOT TO FOLLOW MY **TEACHINGS**.

N.B.

JURASSIK DIARIES

21ST JULY

It's hard to make prehistoric animals, who don't even know what Netflix is, understand glaciation... I have to start with the basics. That's why today I decided to teach them how to write. Now, if you are wondering which fingers they'll do it with, you're just a fussy diary and I don't talk to fussy diaries!
Everyone has a right to education, even dinosaurs.
They will never be able to save themselves from the ice age if they do not understand the consequences and if they cannot read the instructions I will write.

All types of dinosaurs understand me, don't ask me why! Maybe they think I'm the chosen one. I think that I've ended up in the past because their world needs a real hero to change history.

CHAPTER ONE

The smartest dinosaur in the class I teach is LLOYD, a pacifist and vegetarian T-Rex. He dreams of becoming a singer and loves to dress like a pop star. He says that one day he will invent T-rap!

JURASSIK DIARIES

Waldo is a lovely stegosaurus who dreams of flying. It's best not to take him to the mountains, because he might jump into the ravines. He is convinced that all animals can fly. He has never understood how gravity works!

Trisha is a triceratops and she would like to become the president of Jurassika... but she has a pretty bad temper. Let's just say she is easily irritable. Maybe a little too much!

CHAPTER ONE

Of all the other students in my class, Rapto is the velociraptor I enjoy the most. Rapto is the first prehistoric comedian and dreams of acting in a show he is writing called: "Everybody Loves Rapto!" He constantly suffers from a toothache, but that has become part of his show, too.

MEET RAPTO...
TURN THE PAGE!

JURASSIK DIARIES

Of all the other students in my class, the **RAPTO VELOCIRAPTOR** I enjoy the most. Rapto is the first prehistoric comedian and dreams of acting in a live show he is writing called "Everybody Loves Rapto!" He constantly suffers from toothache but that has become part of his show too.

Now, dear diary, you know all about the class I teach... but you still don't know how I got to Jurassika from New York. Please be patient. I will explain it to you, but not today. Right now, I'm sleepy and tomorrow I have a hard day of teaching ahead of me... because there will be the first test of the year.

CHAPTER ONE

22ND JULY

Dear Diary,
I understand that new guests are coming to Jurassika.
It's not easy to grasp everything the pterodactyls say... because of one small detail... they are the only prehistoric animals that don't talk to me!

Noooo! **Noooo!** Noooo!
This is impossible! My worst nightmare is turning into reality!
Mike the bully, along with Ade the henchman and Eve the villain, are here in Jurassika?

JURASSIK DIARIES

Are the biggest bullies from my old school in town? But... how is that possible? Now I'm screwed! Heeeelp!

Heeeelp!

I arrived in Jurassika by mistake. I was going to my grandmother's by bus, I got distracted and I missed the Staten Island bus stop... I got off at the following stop, in Jurassika, even though I didn't know the neighborhood. I thought I would catch another bus from the other side. Instead, in Jurassika there are no buses but only prehistoric animals! This is how I found myself in the past. What if Mike, Ade, and Eve had arrived on the same magic bus that I had taken?

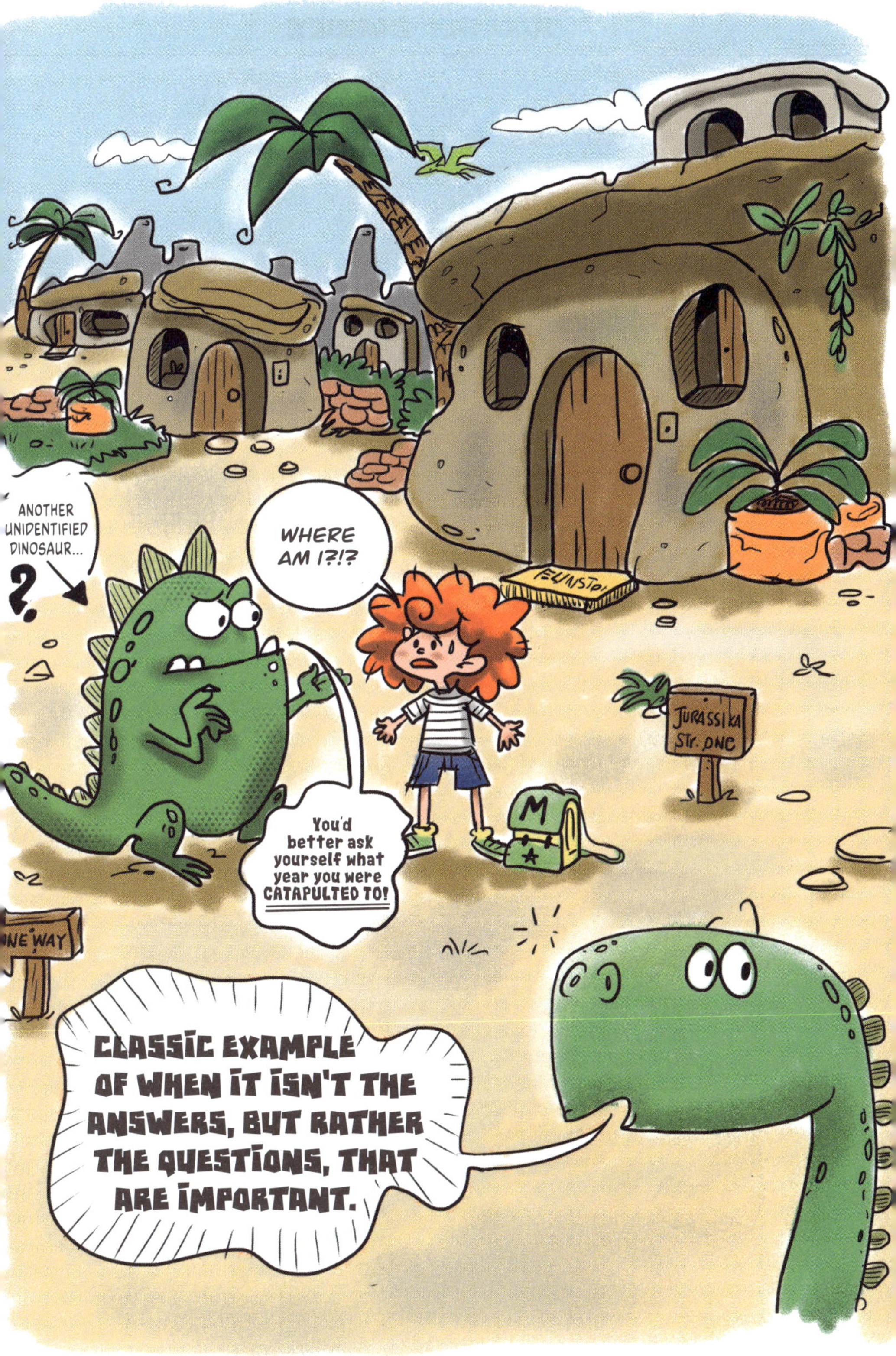
ANOTHER UNIDENTIFIED DINOSAUR...
WHERE AM I?!?
You'd better ask yourself what year you were CATAPULTED TO!
CLASSIC EXAMPLE OF WHEN IT ISN'T THE ANSWERS, BUT RATHER THE QUESTIONS, THAT ARE IMPORTANT.
JURASSIKA STR. ONE

JURASSIK DIARIES

Noooo!

Now they'll bully me, and I won't find the strength for even one of my raspberries! First, I'll be mistreated by them and then I'll get eaten by some T-REX! I'll be the first one of this age to become extinct!

But... if there are no heroes to save me, then I am the hero! It's time to talk to my nice dinosaur friends and ask them for help before Mike and his crew find backup!

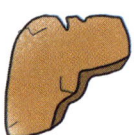 

THE THREE BULLIES

ADE, EVE, AND MIKE. THEY ARE SUCH BULLIES. EVEN THOUGH A BIT...RIDICULOUS. EVE IS SO WICKED THAT SHE INSULTS HERSELF IN THE MIRROR EVERY MORNING. MIKE TELLS A LOT OF LIES AND TOLD HIS PARENTS THAT HE IS THE BEST IN THE CLASS. EVEN THOUGH HE STILL HASN'T FIGURED OUT WHICH CLASS IS HIS! ADE JUST REPEATS WHAT MIKE SAYS AND LAUGHS. LAUGHS AT EVERYTHING. EVEN AT HIMSELF. OF COURSE IF MIKE TELLS HIM TO!

CHAPTER ONE

Bullies are ruthless and brainless. They only have fun when bothering people who are smarter than them. But if they are here to intimidate me, they can't! I am ready to face them. Here, in Jurassika, the one who has the intelligence to create technology wins...and I know how to invent...how to invent...how to invent a rocket to move to another planet!

What am I saying?! Maybe I need a little help from my students... even though they don't seem very gifted to me!

CHAPTER TWO
Here comes the bad guy!

Dear Diary,
The Jurassic world needs a store like Amazon. However, it would be difficult to open an online shop without first inventing a personal computer. What does all this have to do with tyrannosaurs? Nothing!

You always need a computer. Maybe I could watch Netflix after the Pterosaur fights. I'd have to invent the wheel first. But before that, I must try to talk to tyrannosaurs to make them believe that they are vegetarians. It shouldn't be that difficult! Why did they join forces with the bullies?

JURASSIK DIARIES

As soon as they arrived in Jurassika, Mike, Ade, and Eve started bullying little brontosauruses. That's why the Tyrannosaurs liked them right away.

Most T-Rexes love bullying.
As soon as they are born, their parents teach them how to annoy all the other dinosaurs.
They also invented a super mean sport: it's called bullyball. The rules of the game are simple: T-Rexes must hit the heads of brontosaurus with a club!
They aren't exactly known for their intelligence!
Mr. No, the leader of all the T-Rexes, is a rather funny dinosaur, and is known for mostly saying "No!"

CHAPTER TWO

When he first saw Mike, Eve, and Ade, he admired how mean they were, and he said to them: "I like you! That's why I'm going to eat you in one bite. I won't make you suffer!"
Mr. No has a strange idea of kindness, I know!
From what the Pterodactyls reported to me, Mike was able to win over the T-Rexes with his greatest asset: his mobile phone.
Yes, you heard it right! All he needed to do was to show it to them, and those big heads decided to adopt them rather than tear them to pieces.

Mr. No is crazy and a bully, but he's always been a curious guy. He tried to play Crash, and, after an hour, he couldn't do without it. He had become a Nerdosaurus!
That's why the T-Rex decided not to kill the bullies and make them part of his club.

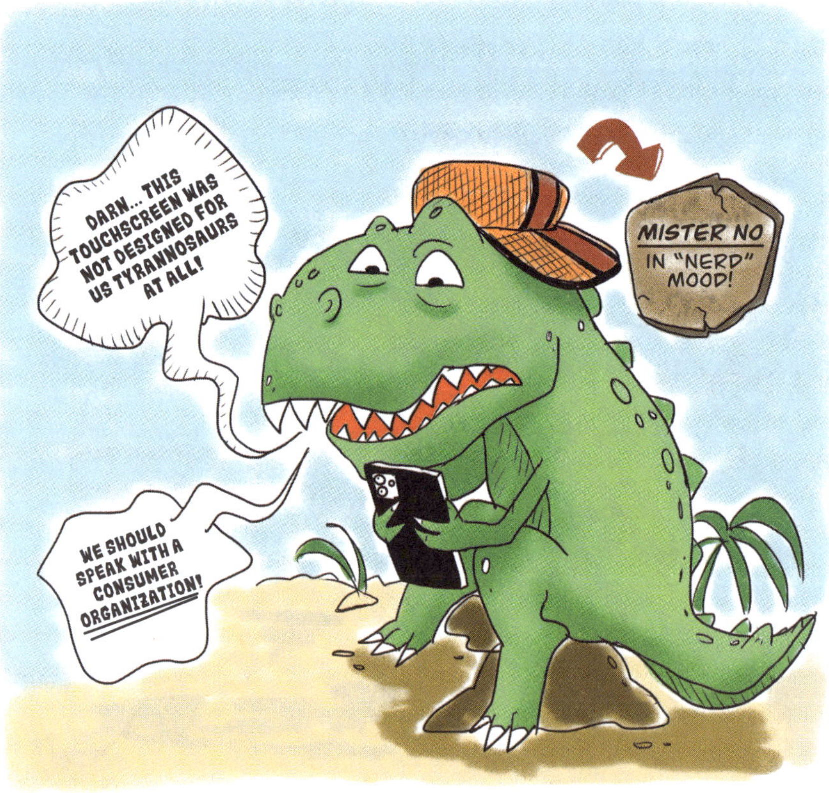
DARN... THIS TOUCHSCREEN WAS NOT DESIGNED FOR US TYRANNOSAURS AT ALL!
WE SHOULD SPEAK WITH A CONSUMER ORGANIZATION!
MISTER NO
IN "NERD" MOOD!

Are you wondering which club I'm talking about?
You don't know the T-Rex club?
Well, where do you live? In the Paleolithic?
Yes, on second thought, you do live in the Paleolithic!

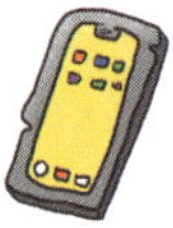

CHAPTER TWO

Mr. No founded the "Darkists" club as soon as I arrived and, when he gathers with his friends, he doesn't spend his time reciting poetry.

THE DARKISTS!
THEY ARE THE WORST!

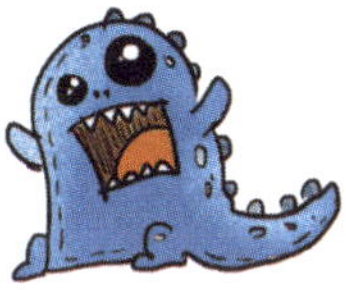

The Darkists, despite what you might think, do not enjoy turning off the lights, because in prehistoric times there are no such things as light bulbs.
They are called "darkists" because they love to gather at night, in the dark, when the moon is up in the sky, and they plot against me.
Why? All of them think that the ice age is just a lie.
They think I tell a lot of lies. According to these grown up lizards, me, the genius, the coolest, the most handsome of the handsome, me who could have been one of the Beatles, a Spice Girl and even Travis Scott, I lie about the end of the Jurassic world. Why don't they understand that I hold the knowledge and the wisdom?
I read! I am the future! Does it take much to understand that? If you met me, wouldn't you ask me for an autograph? Of course! How could you resist my charm?

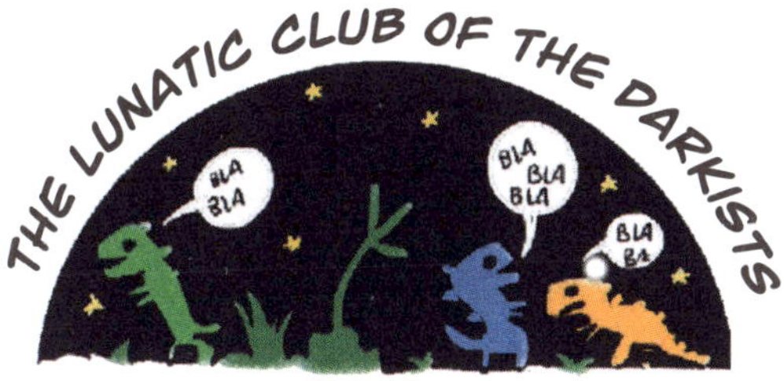
THE LUNATIC CLUB OF THE DARKISTS
BLA BLA
BLA BLA BLA

MARTIN... NARCISSIST?

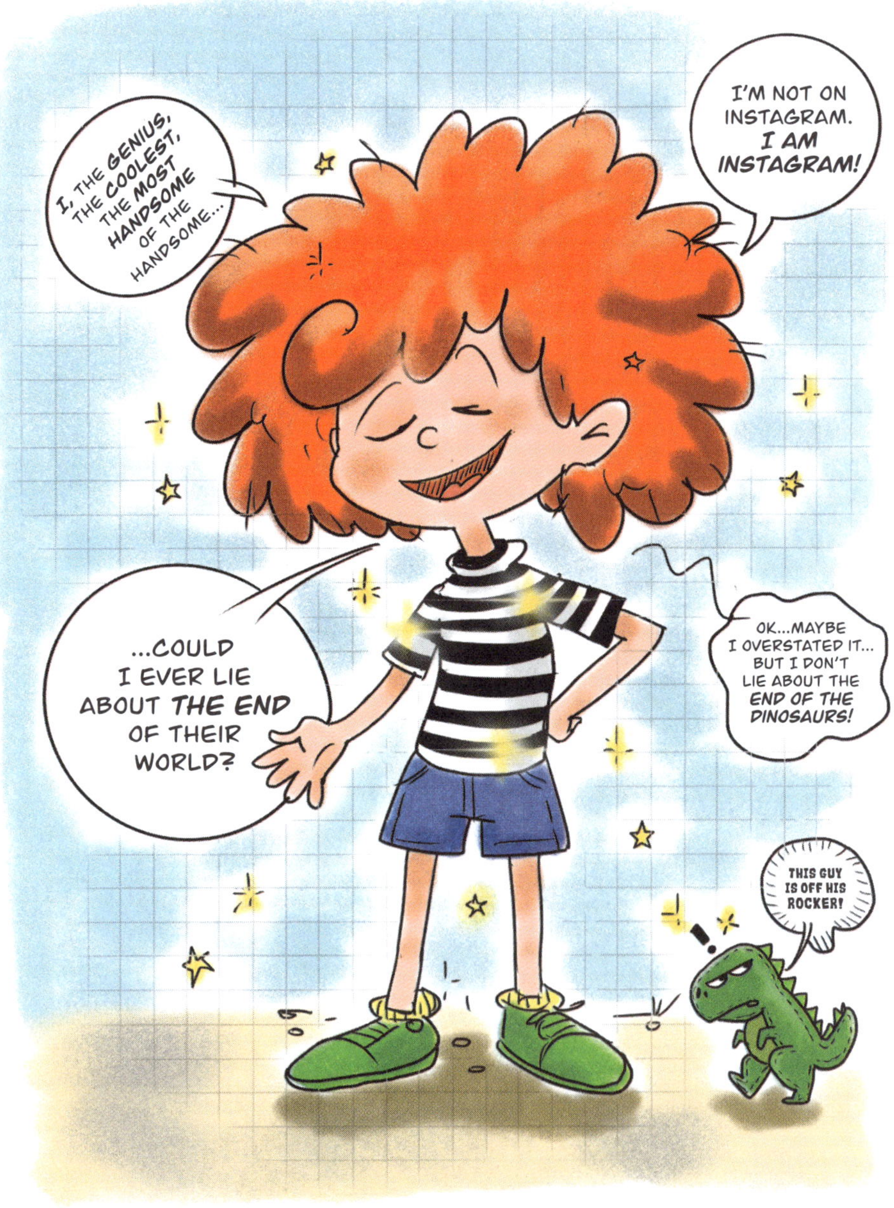
I, THE GENIUS, THE COOLEST, THE MOST HANDSOME OF THE HANDSOME...
I'M NOT ON INSTAGRAM. I AM INSTAGRAM!
...COULD I EVER LIE ABOUT THE END OF THEIR WORLD?
OK...MAYBE I OVERSTATED IT... BUT I DON'T LIE ABOUT THE END OF THE DINOSAURS!
THIS GUY IS OFF HIS ROCKER!

CHAPTER TWO

15TH JULY

Dear Diary, now that the evil Tyrannosaurs have teamed up with the bullies. I am trying to bring knowledge into this world that isn't all that complicated. For example: I spent two hours trying to help Trisha understand what Nutella is. What kind of world do they live in?

Only if they evolve will they be saved.
I have a perfect plan in mind to rescue them and, to implement it, I need them to learn and to understand.
I cannot help them if they do not learn.

THEY NEED MY INTELLIGENCE!

JURASSIK DIARIES

Today I want to test their culture... otherwise it will be very complicated to make them understand and realize my brilliant plan. Lloyd is not like the other tyrannosaurs, he can be understanding, and he is also very intelligent. His artistic flair makes him special. Even though he is the least attentive of my students, I want him to tell me everything he knows. That is why I have prepared an entrance exam for the project: "We will not become extinct."

CHAPTER TWO

I push him, as any good teacher like me would do.
"Come on, Lloyd, concentrate, it's not hard, they are the three objects on which the world has been developed. If you don't know these, how can we hope to fight the ice age?" Lloyd answers me saying that the fire is a stain, the wheel is a hole, and the PS controller is an ice cream.
He's confused.
Really confused, I'd say!
I ask the rest of the class, nobody can answer me.
Rapto is a born comedian and raises his velociraptor paw.

JURASSIK DIARIES

I ask him if he has the answers, he approaches the desk with his microphone and, as if he were in one of those Netflix comedy shows, he says: "Do you want to know a joke backwards? Start laughing!"

DON'T THROW THE COLANDER AWAY!

A social message!

I must begin to educate them and bring them into an evolved age. Am I or am I not the Chosen One?

CHAPTER TWO

That is why I think it's time for the prehistoric world to discover fire. You can warm up with fire...

You can eat with fire.

JURASSIK DIARIES

You can light up the night with fire.

Why is everyone looking at me so scared?
They can't even understand what fire could really be like. The whole class sees it as a special effect, like in the Marvel movies.
They have never seen it and can't understand what I told them. The fire could also be used to signal, but to whom and what? I am trying to make them understand that it could also be useful to dry clothes more quickly...ah, right, they don't have those. So, I'll stop talking.
But how do you create a fire without lighters and matches? I ponder and think that the only way to make them learn about fire is to just show them!

CHAPTER TWO

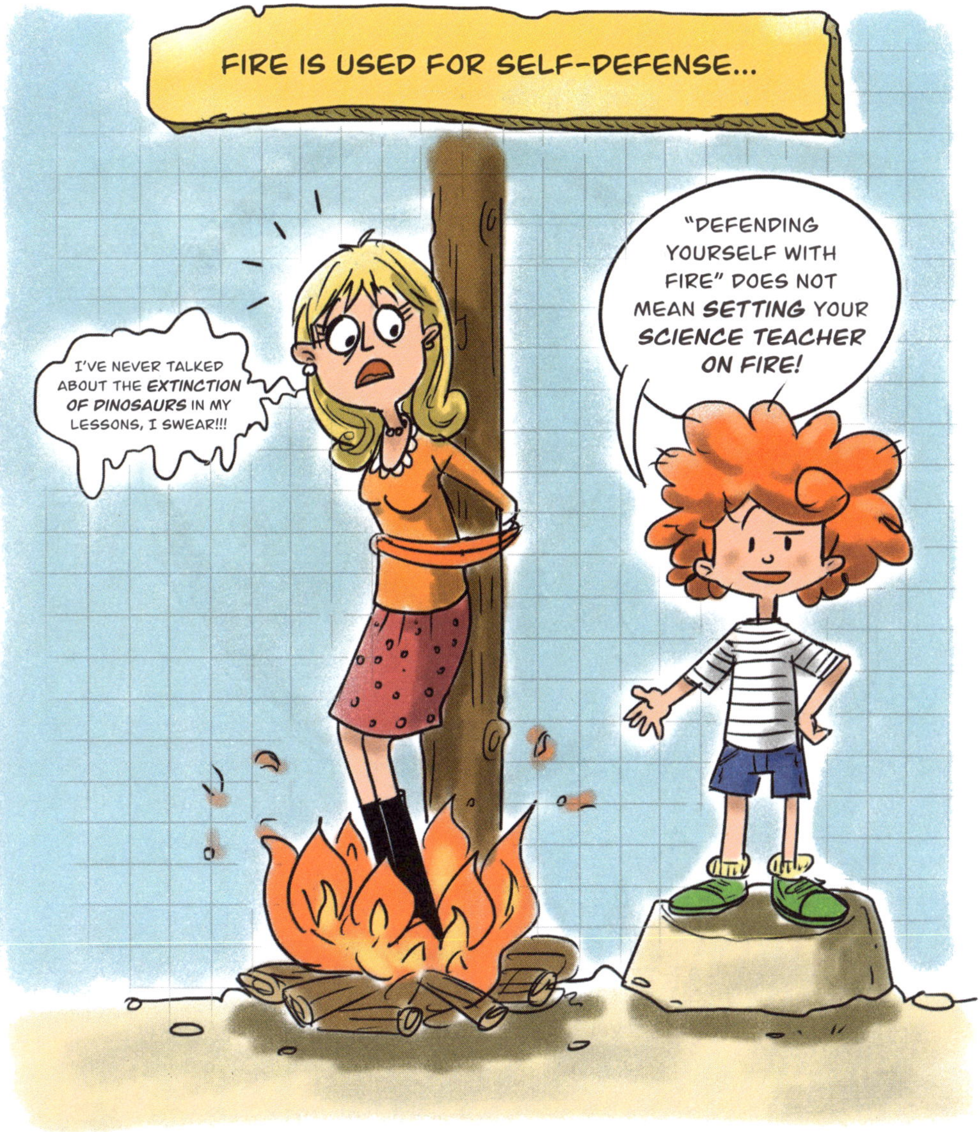
FIRE IS USED FOR SELF-DEFENSE...
I'VE NEVER TALKED ABOUT THE EXTINCTION OF DINOSAURS IN MY LESSONS, I SWEAR!!!
"DEFENDING YOURSELF WITH FIRE" DOES NOT MEAN SETTING YOUR SCIENCE TEACHER ON FIRE!

RULES TO KEEP IN MIND!

I have a very interesting mind, everyone knows that, and I have to think of a solution.

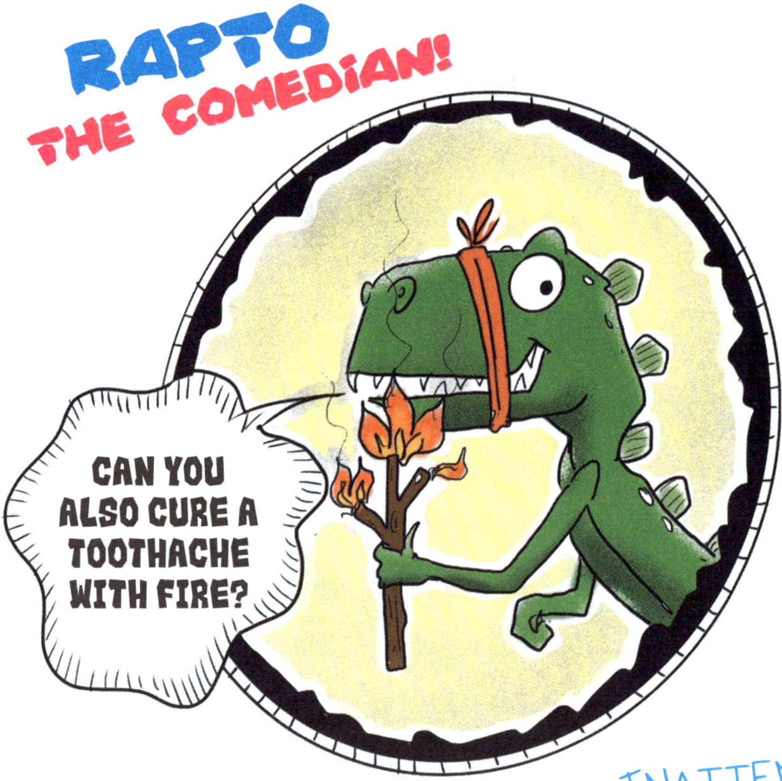
RAPTO THE COMEDIAN!
CAN YOU ALSO CURE A TOOTHACHE WITH FIRE?

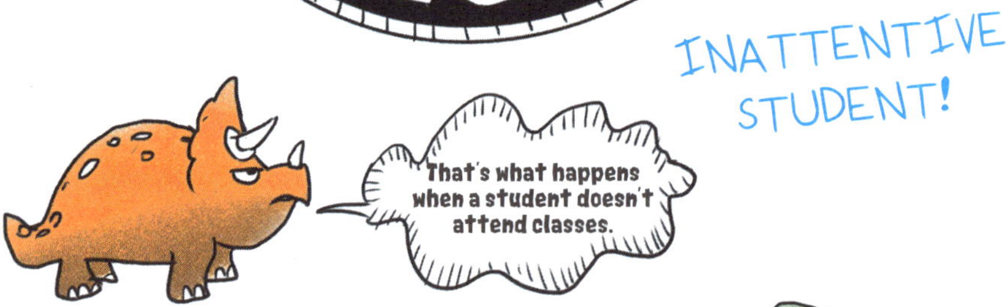
INATTENTIVE STUDENT!
That's what happens when a student doesn't attend classes.

That's what happens when a student doesn't attend classes. Of course, I have my smart-student glasses somewhere in my backpack...

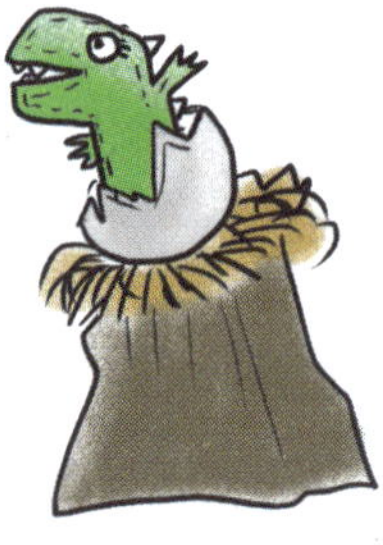

CHAPTER TWO

I usually use them only when my eyes water after hours spent in front of the computer, but in Jurassika I don't have this kind of problem. When the sun is very hot, I can use them to my advantage, thanks to the lenses.
Lighting the fire with this method is not easy, it requires patience. I take the whole class outside the school, put a leaf on the ground and wait for the sun to come through the lens.
It's hot...

HISTORICAL MOMENTS TO REMEMBER!

JURASSIK DIARIES

Luckily, the dry leaf suddenly catches fire and I immediately add more so that the flames are fueled and become more powerful. I expect everyone to be surprised, but when I look at my friends... they are scared and hysterical. Rapto shows his teeth, starts running and shouting: "The new technology will lead us to extinction!!"

CHAPTER TWO

Yet Rapto knows that the best way to show his teeth is with a smile.
The other dinosaurs in the group are also quite dazed.
Lloyd plays his electric guitar loudly and when I ask him not to deafen us, he replies: "I don't want to hear that diabolical noise. I would rather play some Heavy Metal so I don't have to hear that rustling anymore!"
Trisha is silent for the first time ever and I'm worried. I don't want her to be alarmed.

I DON'T WANT HER TO BE ALARMED!!!

She takes a breath and whispers to me: "Can you really cook, warm up, and make light with fire? How can it do all these things together?"
"Mysteries of technology!" I answer her jokingly, but she takes me seriously.
I should maybe learn to keep quiet.
A moment later, I resume thinking I am cool because I am cool!
I was cool in the modern world and I am cool now.

I AM...I AM COOL!

JURASSIK DIARIES

Any doubts?
How can planet Earth resist my charm?
The students of my class don't stand out for their courage nor for their brilliance, but I will make them special. With them I will fight the darkists and together we will save the world from the glaciation. I have the muscles of Conan the Barbarian, the irony of Spider-man, the agility of Black Panther, the intelligence of Professor X, how can I fail to win against the darkists?
Too bad that when I see the shadow of my hair on the ground, I think it's a giant spider and I start running away, terrified!
"Help, a giant spider!!!! A terrible, prehistoric spider!"

IT TAKES A LOT OF *IMAGINATION* TO MISTAKE THE SHADOW OF YOUR HAIR FOR A GIANT SPIDER!

CHAPTER TWO

Everybody laughs because I'm afraid of my shadow, but even the greatest heroes can be afraid.
I feel that it's time for my speech, I must re-establish my authority and make everyone understand who is in charge. "You still have a lot of things to learn, and some of them are essential. It is difficult to explain to you that half of the happiness of the human race comes from a shopping mall and the other half from social networks, but I can explain to you that thanks to the fire we can defend ourselves from the darkists during the night."
I was waiting for a round of applause that didn't happen and, so as to not show my disappointment, I said: "Thank you!" anyway.
I see them confused, as if I were speaking a different language from theirs. Lloyd sits with his guitar in his hand and asks me: "What if I record a song, will I become a T-Rec?"
That should be a joke, but I find it more depressing than a booger stuck under a school desk.

JURASSIK DIARIES

I carry on with my speech and explain: "We now have the fire... we can defend our village and have time to prepare a plan to fight the glaciation. We must be united and there must be many of us!" Waldo is perplexed! Maybe he has a different solution in mind. I see the intelligence in his eyes and ask him: "Would you like to tell us what you are thinking? Maybe you have found a way not to end up frozen?"
Waldo climbs up on the desk, as if he wanted to jump down and fly, and says: "Why is our history book small?"
"Because we're still in prehistoric times!" I shout at him!

AND THIS IS... THE HISTORY BOOK? BUT DIDN'T MARTIN... FEEL LIKE WRITING... BY ANY CHANCE?

WALDO DOESN'T KNOW THAT *HISTORY* HAS YET TO BEGIN!

CHAPTER TWO

I gather strength when a pterodactyl approaches me and says: "Mmfspdjls!"
My goodness!
This time it was very clear to me... I possess a superior intelligence than the average dinosaur, of course!
"What did he say?" Trisha asks me.
"Come on, tell us!
Or maybe it's a secret you want to hide from us?"

I muster the courage and tell everyone what the pterodactyl said. "The darkists have filled the city with posters and are enlisting everyone into their club."
We walk around and we are speechless when we see the T-REX poster.

THE DARKISTS' POSTER

GLACIATION IS AN INVENTION!
JOIN THE DARKISTS AND LET'S ALL FIGHT AGAINST MARTIN!

Soon there will be few of us left to fight against extinction.
I kneel down on the ground in epic style, as if I were in a TV series, shouting to my friends: "We will win against them and after the ice age has passed, we will be the first to say 'It's so hot!'"
Trisha comes up to me with a nice smile and says: "Now that we have discovered fire, why can't we burn the T-Rex posters?"
I would like to explain to her that democracy is about respecting ideas other than one's own, that perhaps a poster only expresses a different point of view, but since I am Martin and I do not like to be contradicted, I rejoice and say: "Great idea! Let's go and turn all the darkists' posters to ashes!"
But when I turn around, I find myself in front of Mr. No. He is with Ade, Mike, and Eve and, with his terrifying grin, he says to me: "You're not going anywhere!"
I think it's time to invent the wheel!

HEEEEEEELP!

GLACIATION IS AN INVENTION!
NOW THAT WE HAVE DISCOVERED FIRE, WHY CAN'T WE BURN THE T-REX POSTERS?

CHAPTER THREE
The world's engine

Chapter 3

Dear Diary,

Mr. No and the darkists chase me while Mike, Eve, and Adam are enjoying it. They have a lot of laughs and they think that being associated with more mischievous and stronger bullies is even more fun than being bullies. Mike laughs and says to Adam: "Sometimes I wish I had teeth like tyrannosaurus' teeth, too!" Adam, who isn't that bright, tries to console him, but he doesn't succeed at all and says: "Your breath stinks like a T-Rex's. It's a good start anyway!"

Eve shakes her head and with her slingshot throws an apple at both of them.

When she is certain that she has almost smashed their heads, she smiles with her Maleficent grin and says: "Now I understand the force of gravity!"

DARKIST BULLIES... YUCK!

JURASSIK DIARIES

I run and I'm short of breath, just like I am short on the hope of saving myself.
I bend over and Mr. No and his henchmen surround me.
I'm doomed!
I must think of a solution.
I look up and say to the flying pterodactyls: "Mnksfakja sfnsk skjf!" They nod and leave.
Obviously, only they and I understand what I say...not you!
So, have patience if you want to know what I said to them. Mr. No is quite puzzled and with his short arms he shows me how his nails shine in the sunlight.
"Time for a showdown!"
I need some time...and so, with all my intelligence, I create my super raspberry!

PRRRRRRR!!!!

This will keep them quiet until the pterodactyls arrive.

PRRRRRRR!!!!
PRRRRRRR!!!!
PRRRRRRR!!!!
PRRRRRRR!!!!

CHAPTER THREE

MARTIN'S INTELLIGENCE CAN BE SEEN FROM AFAR

A GREAT RASPBERRY!!!

JURASSIK DIARIES

Mr. No is laughing his head off... and so are all his "nice" friends from the club.

Mike understood my plan, so he approaches the T-Rexes and shouts to them: "Get up! Don't you understand that the raspberry is his plan to escape? He always has brilliant ideas, that brat!"

But the Tyrannosaurs are not able to recover from the laughter. Mike and his crew throw glasses of water in the darkists' faces.

In the meantime, I leave and start running back to Jurassika. The pterodactyls, just like I told them to, fly close to the T-Rexes, they take a Rubik's cube out of my school bag and throw it at Mr. No's head.

THE RUBIK'S CUBE WORKS MIRACLES...

CHAPTER THREE

"Oooouuuch!" cries annoyed Mr. No, who grabs the cube in his hand and tries to understand what it is.
"Play, play!" he repeats after a few seconds, he sits down on the ground and so do all the other tyrannosaurs.
Mike goes nuts and tries to make the darkists understand that I have escaped.
"You can't play now! Martin has escaped!"
Mr. No doesn't worry though and, with his gaze fixed on the cube, he repeats: "Play, Play!"
I arrive in the village and lock myself in the school. I call the whole class together and explain to them my formidable new ideas.
"There are few of us and we will hardly win a battle against the darkists.
They have convinced many animals to follow them and so the time has come for me to amaze the whole Prehistory with a great invention! Indeed, with two great inventions! Everyone will have to understand that I have the technology and the knowledge and therefore I am the only one able to save the world!"
Of course, I know I'm a bit presumptuous, but big leaders always have a big ego. Or don't they? Maybe I am confusing them with dictators!
Rapto has his usual toothache and asks me: "I know it has nothing to do with it, but you told us about Adam and Eve... and you said they were born adults. So, they didn't get their baby teeth? Blessed are they!"
I cough and I think that I have to impress my class, because they are getting more and more distracted.

JURASSIK DIARIES

30TH JULY

It's time to amaze them.
I stand in front of the blackboard and draw a Ferrari!
"This is a car and also quite a cool one! We need several of these in order to escape from the bad T-Rexes... they will also take us to new places that we could NOT OTHERWISE get to."
Trisha is perplexed and approaches the desk.
"Martin, shouldn't you invent roads first?"

CHAPTER THREE

WHAT TO INVENT FIRST!

Here we go again!
If I invent the road,
I will have to invent parking lots too!
Maybe the invention of the car can wait. Now I understand the real questions of the world: Was it the road or the car that came first? Was the gasoline or the car created first?
Perhaps I don't know anything about the planet I live on.
But I'm stubborn, and I try to explain to all the dinosaurs what the car really is and why we need it.

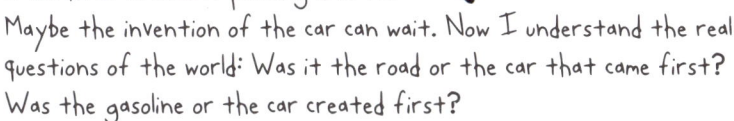

"The car will be fast, so we can overtake everyone,
even the cheetah...and then we can go to the city where
there are no bad animals!"
Waldo swoops onto the desk using a mega slingshot built by him and activated
by Rapto and shatters the entire desk.
He gets up and, as if nothing had happened, he tells me: "Maybe you should
invent the gas pumps first, and also
the mechanics to help us repair the cars in case of a breakdown!"

I must lower my expectations!
The world is not yet ready for my intelligence.
"Guys, forget the car. I suppose it's wise to invent the wheel first. This will allow us to build bicycles and carriages."
Rapto touches his aching teeth and gets closer to me, as I am standing in the center of the class.
"Will we still go faster than the cheetahs?"
I have a good laugh and I answer him as a politician looking for votes would do.
"Of course! The bicycle will transform your lives. You will go very fast! You will be faster than a Ferrari!"

AND NOW I SHOULD INVENT MONEY AND EVEN THE ATM TO PAY FOR THE GASOLINE?!

Has the world been invented all together?

> GO AND CHASE YOUR DREAMS!!!

> HOT-HEADED!

> CLASSIC EXAMPLE OF A WHEEL THAT LEADS NOWHERE...

In the yard in front of the school, we build the first wheel together.
Waldo arrives with a rectangular rock in his mouth, he drops it and asks me:
"Is this one round?"
I raise and wave the signaling disk, with an M on it, in front of his face.
He makes me angry, because he doesn't understand anything,
and I yell at him: "You deserve the M for mediocre!"
Waldo gives me a cunning look, as if it
were me who was wrong.
"You said the wheel is round and this stone is round like the
Earth. Right?" He didn't really understand
anything.

CHAPTER THREE

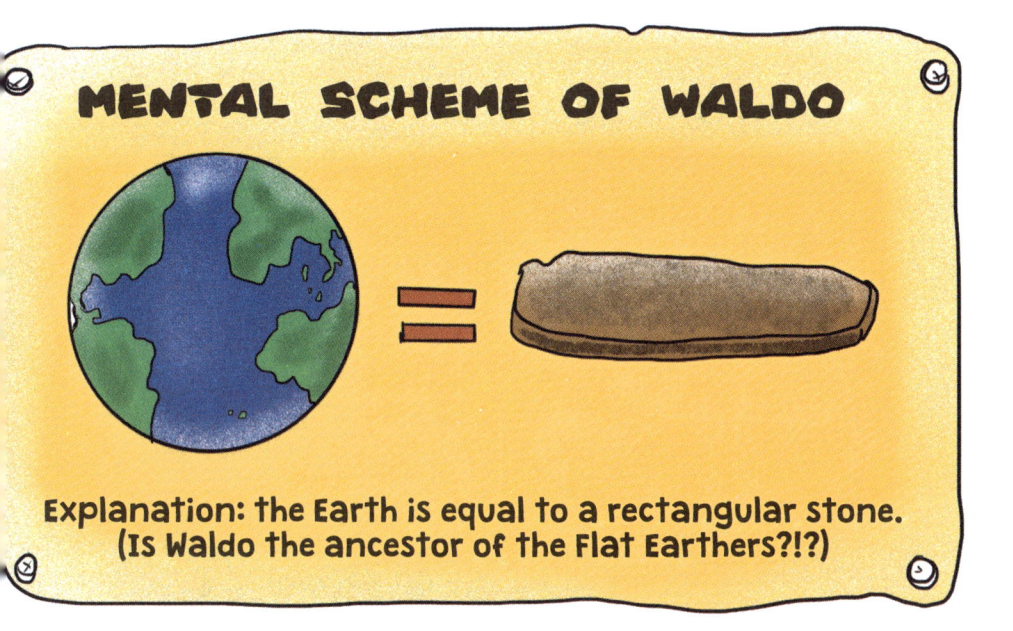

MENTAL SCHEME OF WALDO

Explanation: the Earth is equal to a rectangular stone. (Is Waldo the ancestor of the Flat Earthers?!?)

I build the bicycle and finally insert two round stones in where the tires go. At least I'm sure they won't get punctured.
Waldo and Trisha look at me confused.
Trisha decides to get on the bike but falls on the ground. She hurts herself and asks me: "Why wouldn't you invent a bicycle with four wheels?"
Then I understand that the bicycle is no good either!

THE ADVENTURES OF MARTIN BY BIKE

WALDO, TRISHA, LOOK AT ME... WITH NO HANDS!

WALDO, TRISHA, LOOK AT ME... WITH NO FEET!

DARN...!

WALDO... TRISHA...LOOK AT ME...GULP... WITH NO TEETH...!

Such an ugly comic...

CHAPTER THREE

I have an idea and I want to talk to Rapto about it. However, where is he?
I look around and I don't see him. I hope he hasn't gone off to play hide and seek. Right now, we have to get organized because our enemies could come back at any moment. Trisha and Waldo are also worried about Rapto. He usually complains about his teeth all the time. I hope he will stop playing and come out of some bush.
"Rapto! Where are you?"
I scream desperately. He is the funniest of the gang.
The pterodactyls approach and I ask them if they have seen Rapto.
"Hsif jassfl s jfsso jfs!" they answer me. Hmmmmm...
We really didn't need this!

DO YOU WANT TO FIND OUT WHAT HAPPENED TO RAPTO? LEAF THROUGH THE PAGES OF MY DIARY!

WHERE IS RAPTO?

CHAPTER FOUR
Troy's T-Rex

Chapter 9

"It was the bullies! Yes, the bullies and the T-Rexes kidnapped Rapto!" I explain to my friends. That's what the pterodactyls told me. "Noooo!!" cries Waldo. Trisha grinds her teeth and says: "We'll show them!" My brain springs into action, and

I understand everything...as always! But of course! I know why they have kidnapped our friend.

"Waldo and Trisha, listen to me! They have kidnapped Rapto because they hope to discover what new invention I'm going to create, so the bullies will invent the solution first and then they will attack us... perhaps in the middle of the night."

DOC, HOW LONG CAN A BRAINLESS PERSON LIVE?

I DON'T KNOW...HOW OLD ARE YOU?

A classic example of someone who uses his brain badly!

JURASSIK DIARIES

Trisha puts on an eye patch, and I look at her perplexed.
"What did you put on your face?"
It looks like something out of an action movie.
"Now I am ready to go to war! Isn't an eye patch enough to make you look more evil?"
I smile because she wouldn't look evil even with the face of a T-Rex.
Waldo raises his hand, even though we're not in class: "Little Prof, what do you want to do?"
"Definitely don't wait for them!"
"What does that mean?"
"I have a great plan in mind, and we'll call it the Trojan T-Rex!"
"What?"
Waldo's eyes are frightened. His brain doesn't work as fast as mine.

I AM MARTIN'S BRAIN AND THE TRUTH IS THAT I ABANDONED HIM BECAUSE I UNDERSTOOD WHO I WAS DEALING WITH!

CHAPTER FOUR

"I will be like Ulysses... you, Waldo, will be Epeo and Trisha will be Athena!" My friends don't understand me. They think I'm speaking in a code language, instead I'm just exhibiting my great literary knowledge. It's time to take them back to class and explain my project on the blackboard, maybe they won't look at me as if I was the only cat in the kennel.
"Do you trust my genius?" I ask them. They don't answer me. I take that as a yes!

JURASSIK DIARIES

I'm in front of the desk and I have drawn on the blackboard a perfect horse, that whoever illustrates my diary drew very poorly (you need to be patient!). "The Trojan horse is a war machine that, according to legend, was used by the Greeks to take over the city of Troy. After ten long years of siege, the Greeks implement a plan devised by Ulysses. They leave the beach in front of Troy, where they abandon a huge wooden horse built by Epeo with the help of Athena. They go hiding on the nearby island of Tenedo, pretending to return home. Inside the horse, however, they leave some of the most valiant warriors of Agamemnon, led by Ulysses himself."

Waldo raises his hand and asks me: "What if we squashed a horse, wouldn't it be faster?"
These prehistoric animals do not seem evolved at all to me.

CHAPTER FOUR

"Of course not!" I say annoyed, "We must build a big horse that you will offer as a gift to the darkists. I'll be the great warrior who will hide inside the wooden animal that we build, and at night, when Mr. No and the darkists are asleep, I will set Rapto free!"
"So, we need to build a horse?" Trisha asks me.
"Sort of!"
"How?"
"We will not offer them a horse! We are going to gift them a big wooden T-Rex!"

LUCKILY THE T-REXES HAVE SHORT ARMS... WE'RE ALMOST OUT OF WOOD!

"You are a genius! Your ideas are unique!" he says smiling.
I've just brought back an old story that I studied in school, but I know that it is new to the Jurassic world, and also to bullies... Do you know why? Because they have never opened a schoolbook. I will also win this battle because culture always wins over ignorance.

Hours go by and the three of us work hard to finish the "Trojan T-Rex." We're tired, so tired that if I had to sleep, I wouldn't need to count any dream sheep.
I sit on the floor and admire the huge wooden T-Rex and at that point Waldo comes closer and asks me: "Martin, were you serious? Will you be the great warrior who will hide inside?"
I look around and answer with confidence: "Do you see someone else around who is strong and brave?"
"No! I actually don't see anyone!"
He seems to think it's impossible that a genius can also be strong.

SCIENTIFIC DILEMMA:
If man descends from the monkey, who does the monkey descend from? Better not to think about it... I have to save my brain for the important things: like eating pizza!

I DISCOVERED THAT FOR...NOM... EATING A... NOM... PIZZA... NOM... YOU USE 39 MUSCLES...
SO... GOODBYE GYM.
PIZZA

JURASSIK DIARIES

Yes, I confess that my muscles are not "traditional," so let's call them "differently strong."
Yet this will not make me a less credible warrior.
I'm Martin, Martin Little Brain, I know it's an absurd surname, but it's who I am and I'm not ashamed of it. These are the contradictions of life!
I call Waldo and Trisha and say, "I know what I'm doing, and I'll bring Rapto back home!"

MARTIN HAS A STRANGE IDEA OF MUSCLES

> BOTTOM LINE: WE MUST TRAIN A LOT TO LEARN HOW TO LISTEN!

> I TRAIN THE SMALLEST MUSCLES OF THE HUMAN BODY: THE EARS! OBVIOUSLY!

> WHAT ARE YOU DOING?

Before I get inside the Trojan T-Rex, I look at the sky. A strange cloud is hanging over our heads. It's dark and seems to be heavy. Suddenly, an icy wind blows over us.

CHAPTER FOUR

Snowflakes start to fall on our heads.
Waldo and Trisha look at them as if they were tiny alien spaceships. "What are they?" asks Trisha with eyes as huge as two hot-air balloons.
They are not familiar with snow and that means that something horrible will be coming soon... the glaciation is showing its first signs.
I muster the courage and think of the right words to use, because I don't want to frighten my friends.
I think about it for a few minutes, because I must find the least harsh way to tell them the truth. I breathe in and say: "Guys, what's falling on your head is... DEATH!!! The glaciation is about to begin! You will end up like icicles if you don't listen to me!"
Perhaps I exaggerated a little bit. Yes, I'm sure that I exaggerated! In fact, Waldo and Trisha fall on the ground. They have fainted. I throw water on their faces and they come to their senses. "Come on, let's look at the positive side of things. Soon, you will understand what refrigerators are!"

67

JURASSIK DIARIES

I know, I could have saved myself such an idiotic joke, but my brain often speaks loudly by itself.

BLAH BLAH BLAH

Trisha gets up and wants to proudly make one thing clear: "I'll be the one to give our 'Trojan T-Rex' to those bragging darkists."
"How do we push this huge wooden object to the T-Rexes?" Waldo asks me.
"We'll put some wheels underneath and push it!" I answer him.
At last I see his eyes glowing with intelligence, and he says:
"Of course, with wheels!"
Waldo, after a few minutes, assembles two triangular stones under the T-Rex, and I understand that he hasn't learned anything at all so far!

REMEMBER: THE WHEEL IS ROUND!

OF COURSE I KNOW WHAT A WHEEL IS! ALL WHEELS HAVE 3 SIDES AND 3 CORNERS!

THIS IS A TRIANGLE.

(P.S., He will learn sooner or later!)

CHAPTER FOUR

We wait for night to fall on Jurassika and the village of the darkists. We light a fire to find our way and we whisper so that the darkists don't hear us... we arrive in Rex Burg, the village where the bad tyrannosaurs and bullies live. They surrounded their caves with a wooden fort.
They have protection from any kind of attack, at least that's what they think.
We wait for the sun to come back up in the sky and when the T-Rexes on guard duty become visible, Trisha approaches the big door and rings the bell, which is nothing but the nose of a poor brontosaurus held prisoner. The brontosaurus screams and so Gin and Seng, the two T-Rexes on watch, open the doors and walk towards Trisha.

JURASSIK DIARIES

"Who are you?" shouts Gin.
Trisha smiles and recites the story she has carefully prepared.
"I am a fan of Mr. No!"
"A fan of Mr. No?" asks Seng intrigued. It is the first time he sees a triceratops cheering for a T-Rex.
"He is mighty, the best, the meanest and the most ignorant! How could I not love him? He has brought fear to our village and I have been fascinated by it."
The two guards look each other in the eyes and smile.
"What do you want from our great leader?"
Trisha smiles, because she had anticipated that question.
"It will be Christmas in a few days... and he will receive a lot of gifts from Santa Claus, but nothing like this big wooden sculpture. It wouldn't fit in the fireplace or the door. I want him to be happy and to have a great gift, just like his enormous wickedness."

CHRISTMAS IS COMING
CHRISTMAS
PRESENTS PRESENTS
PRESENTS PRESENTS
PRESENTS PRESENTS
PRESENTS PRESENTS
PRESENTS PRESENTS
PRESENTS PRESENTS

CHAPTER FOUR

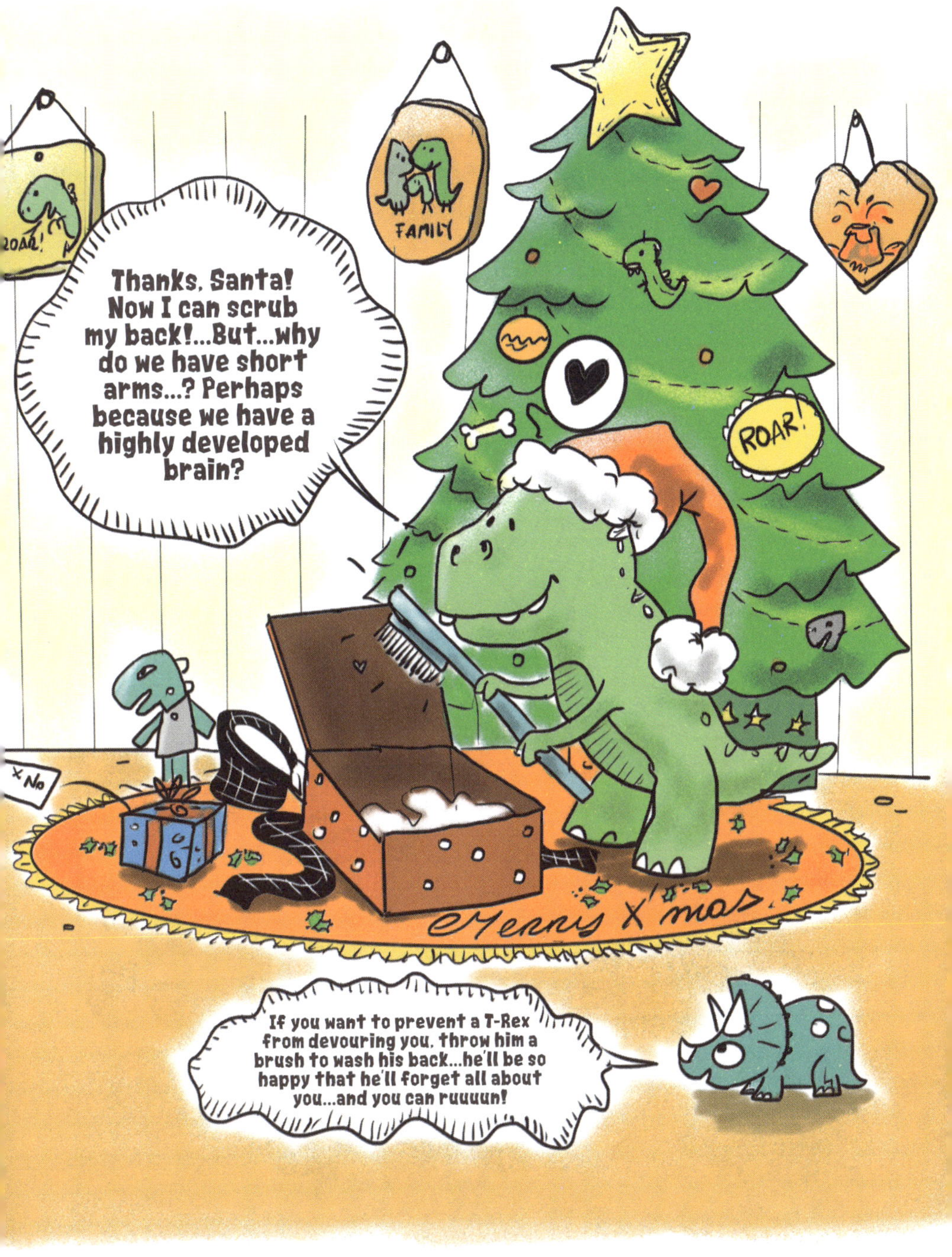

JURASSIK DIARIES

Gin skips because he has a gift for his boss and Seng brings out his sharp teeth to Trisha and says, "You are a good subject. So, as a gift, we will leave you free to go back to your village and live in terror for the next few years." "How kind you are!" Trisha replies sarcastically, but the tyrannosaurs don't understand that she is pretending to appreciate their words, "Today you won't tear me to pieces and this is my FANTASTIC Christmas present. You are wonderful animals!"
The two guards blush, as if Trisha was really impressed by their goodness.

CHAPTER FOUR

"Could I say hello to Mr. No?" asks Trisha.
Gin approaches the movable sculpture and he shakes his head.
"No one can enter the city. But your T-Rex will be brought to him."
Trisha says goodbye with a smile and, before leaving, says: "Give my gift to Mr. No! His wickedness is unique, and that makes him the most wicked among the wicked."
Gin and Seng are moved. They are not used to hearing the oppressed thrilled to be dominated by the evil ones.
They take the "Trojan T-Rex" and drag it into the city.
In the meantime, Trisha meets Waldo, who is waiting for her hidden behind a rock.
"Now it's Martin's turn!" says Trisha. Waldo trusts me, and reassures her: "Martin is a hero and will save Rapto!"

No! Wait, go back. That's not exactly how it happened.
"Now it's Martin's turn!" says Trisha.
Waldo trusts me, and reassures her: "Martin sucks as a hero, but something will happen that will save Rapto! We believe in luck!"

The ancient hero is the one who fought for his people. The modern hero is the one who fights with his PlayStation!

Martin the Gladiator!

Are we sure this guy understood that he must save Rapto from the darkists?

JURASSIK DIARIES

> WHERE AM I GOING? WHERE DID THEY HIDE RAPTO? AND WHO KNOWS WHAT THE NY METS ARE DOING RIGHT NOW? INTELLIGENT PEOPLE ARE ALWAYS FULL OF DOUBTS... THEY SAY...

> Even doubts, however, must be intelligent!

It's the dead of night. So it's late.
It's night, we get it!
Some small holes let me glimpse whether there is anyone around.
I hear Mr. No walk by and say to Mike, Eve, and Adam: "I'm glad they're giving me presents because they're afraid of me and not because I deserve them!"
Mr. No's ideas are clear! If his goodness were a tree, it would be a bonsai.
It's time to get out of the "Trojan T-Rex" and go find Rapto.
I look around, it seems that everyone has gone somewhere else and I hear voices coming from far away. I need to go where everyone is and not to be seen, maybe I will find out where they are holding Rapto.

CHAPTER FOUR

The moon is like a spotlight and illuminates all the darkists who are gathered in a circle around Rapto. My friend is locked inside a cage and the others are laughing.
He entertains them with his show and the darkists seem to like his comedy.
I cannot bear to see such a scene.
It reminds me of Celine Dion in Las Vegas.
I have to break him out and bring him back to Jurassika.
Rapto tells a joke: "A snake opens up to a friend. 'Has she left you?' the friend asks him. 'Yes, but I am sure she will slither back...' he replies."
The darkists applaud and giggle.
They have found their free of charge entertainment, because I am certain that they don't know about copyright or the price of the ticket.

THE THREE BULLIES

THE THREE BULLIES ADE, EVE, AND MIKE ARE WEIRD PEOPLE FROM THEIR MIDDLE SCHOOL IN THE MODERN WORLD. YOU HAVE TO KNOW THAT EVE ALWAYS WROTE HER HOMEWORK IN LOWER-CASE HANDWRITING. WHY? BECAUSE SHE THOUGHT THAT MISTAKES WERE LESS NOTICEABLE THAT WAY. ADE WAS ALWAYS ASLEEP AND WHEN THE MATH TEACHER TOLD HIM THAT HE SHOULDN'T SLEEP IN SCHOOL, HE REPLIED: "I KNOW, MRS. TEACHER, IT WOULD BE POSSIBLE IF YOU TALKED A BIT LESS!"

A brontosaurus goes to the doctor and says: Doctor, I think I am invisible! And the doctor replies: Who is speaking?
HA!
HA!
HA!
HA!
HA!
HA!

CHAPTER FOUR

I'm waiting for the show to end and for everyone to go to sleep.
Mike the bully talks to Eve and says: "Rapto is a hoot and entertains all the darkists, we should keep him forever."
Eve starts jumping around and repeating: "Yes, yes!"
When she is happy, Eve does somersaults. And now she is happier than the time she locked one of her classmates in the closet. "Mike," continues Eve, "can I splash some water on his face before going to sleep? I know it bothers him, so we can laugh a bit."
I've never understood bullies. Why do they enjoy humiliating others?
In my opinion, they are like extinguished matches. What do I mean by that? Well, they are perfectly useless.
Ade claps his hands, as if the real show was about to begin.
"Annoyance!
We annoy!
I miss bullying others. Ah, such beautiful memories at school!" says Ade, a little nostalgic.
Eve takes a bottle of water and begins to shake it!
"Yes, there's nothing more fun than being a bully, because the alternative is to be bullied."

MIKE, ADE, AND EVE ARE BULLIES!!
THEY ENJOY BOTHERING PEOPLE!!!!

JURASSIK DIARIES

NICE?
EVA PLAYS WITH A DARKIST!

WOULD YOU LIKE A SOCCER BALL?

YES!

DO YOU PREFER IT IN THE TEETH OR ON THE LEGS?

THAT'S HOW A BULLY HAS FUN!

BULLIES DON'T REALLY KNOW HOW TO KEEP A FRIEND!

CHAPTER FOUR

I have to stop them before they make fun of my friend Rapto.
All the tyrannosaurs attending the show are gone... and the bullies are left alone.
I start using my brain to find a solution, otherwise my friend will be humiliated.
But, of course! I got it!
Fire can do about a thousand things, so I decide to make a flashlight.
Yesterday, by chance, I invented matches while everyone else was sleeping.

MARTIN INVENTS THE MATCHSTICK

1 SAW TEETH ARE SHARPER THAN T-REX TEETH!

2 THICKNESS 2,5 MM

3 AMMONIUM PHOSPHATE

I CUT SOME WOOD INTO MANY THIN BOARDS ABOUT 2.5 MM THICK. I THEN DIVIDED THE BOARDS INTO MANY SMALL STICKS AND IMMERSED EACH STICK (ONLY ONE END) IN A SOLUTION OF AMMONIUM PHOSPHATE.

WANT TO KNOW WHERE MARTIN FOUND THE AMMONIUM PHOSPHATE? DON'T ASK! NOT EVEN PHILIP OSBOURNE KNOWS...HE JUST FOUND IT!

Hey you, reading this crazy story, never try to imitate Marin!

JURASSIK DIARIES

I decide to light the flashlight with a match and scare the T-Rexes. They are afraid of what they don't know and the fire will burn them if they try to get close.

The panic should draw the attention of Ade, Mike, and Eve and so they will have to stop. Then I will save Rapto just like a true hero who helps their defenseless friends.

> WOW, SO MUCH AMMONIUM PHOSPHATE! NOW I CAN BUILD ALL THE MATCHES IN THE WORLD!

Philip Osbourne coudn't help but explain how Martin invented the matchstick. Obviously, you are going to pretend to believe it...otherwise he'll continue for another 60 pages trying to make credible something that is not!

THEY ARE SIMPLE AND COMMON PUDDLES...

CHAPTER FOUR

Except that something is not going according to plan. I try to light the flashlight, but my shirt catches fire instead. Nooo! That's why they say, "Never play with fire!"
Damn it! I start running with my T-shirt on fire and all the T-Rexes mistake me for the human torch. Mr. No, frightened and alarmed, screams to all the darkists: "Run, retreat! The fire from the sky will roast us like chickens on a spit."
Panic ensues and those big, scary villains suddenly look like children frightened by their own shadow.

I AM YOUNG. I STILL HAVE TO GROW UP AND WRITE MY BEST-SELLING NOVEL... I CAN'T DIE BEFORE I'VE WRITTEN IT! I ALREADY HAVE THE TITLE IN MIND.*

MR. NO

*MR. NO'S BOOK

T-NOCCHIO
The story of a lying T-Rex and his fairy

The novel that Mr. No would like to write! Does it remind you of anything?

JURASSIK DIARIES

"Let's go!" I say to Rapto.
I open his cage
and he hugs me and licks my face.
I am happy to see him again. I missed him. "We don't have much time, before they realize that I was not 'the fire from the sky.' Let's run!"
"Thank you for risking your life to save a friend with a toothache."
"Wouldn't you have done the same?" I ask Rapto. He smiles at me, and then, to distract me, he says: "Look how beautiful! A shooting star!"
We run and manage to get out of the village gates.
Waldo and Trisha are waiting for us.
Waldo is so happy to see us, he says: "Climb on top of me and I will take you to Jurassika!"
"Waldo, you are not a pterodactyl!" I remind him, hoping to bring him back to reality.
He smiles at me and sweetly replies:
"I am at heart!"

SUPER RAPTO

DARKISTS NEED ENTERTAINMENT!

THEY KIDNAPPED RAPTO! HOW ARE WE GOING TO LAUGH NOW?! DOES ANYONE HAVE A SUBSCRIPTION TO NETFLIX OR PRIME? WE COULD WATCH A MOVIE WITH ADAM SANDLER, AT LEAST!
MR. NO, WE ARE IN PREHISTORY! RAPTO IS THE ONLY ENTERTAINMENT! BUT IF YOU WANT, I'LL START DANCING!
TYPICAL EXAMPLE OF "WHEN IT RAINS, IT POURS!"

JURASSIK DIARIES

We run and we manage to leave the darkists behind us, who are evil, but not smart.

THEY ARE NOT SMART!

Before they understood our plan, some time has passed.
We are free!

WE ARE FREE!

Finally we will be able to go back to Jurassika and convince as many dinosaurs as possible that glaciation is near.
We can't waste any time, because soon everything will freeze and there will be no more dinosaurs left.
We hear a strange noise coming from the sky.
Fortunately the moon is full and it allows me to see what caused that screeching sound. I am speechless.
A drone in prehistoric times?
What is it doing here?
The drone is carrying a huge box.
What could it be?

amazon
AMAZON IS DELIVERING THE CELL PHONES THAT I REQUESTED...AND NOW WE CAN SUBDUE ALL THE DINOSAURS! ...EVEN MARTIN'S LITTLE FRIENDS!
ADEEEE, YOU STOLE MY ROLE! I'M THE BOSS AND I'M THE ONE WITH BRILLIANT IDEAS!
Take it easy, Mike, or you'll get a blood clot!

JURASSIK DIARIES

How did they get the technology to prehistoric times?
And what do the darkists have in mind? Obviously, keep reading my diary to find out!

29th July!

What do the darkists and bullies have in mind?
I feel that problems are coming.

What was in the package?
The bullies together with the darkists are like gasoline with fire.

Martin, what are you writing?
JURASSIC DIARIES
P. OSBOURNE
!
Leave him alone, dear! Keep reading the story!

CHAPTER FIVE
The importance of a subscription

Chapter 5

2ND AUGUST

It's time to get serious. I don't have any more time to stall. I don't think that the glaciation will send me a message to warn me of its arrival. The dinosaurs' world depends on me and I will save these stupid and horrible creatures. Why would I do that? Because I care about my friends and even those that just don't understand what is happening.

A hero doesn't ask himself who to rescue, but he asks himself: in prehistoric times where do you buy clothes like the super cool guys from Marvel?

I have a perfect plan and I asked Waldo, Trisha, and Rapto to gather all the inhabitants of Jurassika. I will explain to them how they can save themselves. I have created the perfect plan. Strangely enough though, there are only a few people who showed up for my lecture.

Can you hurry? The darkists are giving away some cell phones and you're upsetting me with this glaciation story!

WHY IS EVERYONE LEAVING MY BRILLIANT LECTURE? WHAT IS HAPPENING?

JURASSIK DIARIES

I understand that talking about extinction is not exciting ... but I can't pretend nothing is happening and start selling ice cream, as if the summer lasts forever. Also because the T-Rexes will keep all of the ice cream for themselves.

CHAPTER FIVE

My task is to save these crazy dinosaurs... and I will do it at any cost.
Otherwise I would be a very bad hero.
I ponder over what the brontosaurus told me.
The T-Rexes are giving away cell phones.
Hmmm!
So this is what the drone was carrying: smartphones.
Why are they giving away cell phones?
How did they manage to order them?
This is the bullies' idea, I'm sure.
Maybe they think it's time to subjugate all the dinosaurs on earth and the only way to talk to all of them is through cell phones!
Well, they know that dinosaurs go crazy for video games!
I have to explain my plan to everyone before they can convince every dinosaur that glaciation will never come.

SCIENTIFIC DILEMMA:
What did the first dinosaur do by himself? And did he realize he was a vegetarian after he had eaten some poor animal?

Dear Diary, you should know that dinosaurs go crazy over cell phones, so when they meet, they are not forced to talk to each other. I am convinced that they are looking for an application that will allow them to track animals nearby ready to be eaten.

JURASSIK DIARIES

I'm in class and everyone looks at me with those curious and a little frightened eyes. I have to reassure them I can save them with the perfect plan.
It is time to explain it to them.
"Let's start with the basic rule: the ice age is cold. This means that we must first build a warm place to take refuge."
Waldo raises his paw and asks: "Will we need lots of blankets? I am good at sewing them!"
I laugh because he doesn't realize that the temperature will drop below zero and the blankets won't be enough to protect us against the cold.
"Huge blankets will be needed for the Mammoths, the brontosaurus, and for everyone...but they won't be enough. The cold will make our teeth chatter and will not allow us to move...that's why we will build heated tunnels!"
I show my project on the blackboard: drawings always help make things clear.

HEAT

Will the fire save us from the ice age?

Yes, if we fill the tunnel where we are going to hide with it.

IT WILL BE SO COLD THAT WOLVES WILL EAT SHEEP MERELY FOR THE WOOL!

WE WANT SUMMER!!

MARTIN ALWAYS KNOWS HOW TO REASSURE THE DINOSAURS...

THE PERFECT PLAN OF EVE, ADE, MIKE, AND MR. NO

I HAVE AN IDEA TO DEFEAT MARTIN! WE ALL THINK IT'S NICE TO WAKE UP, REACH OUT, AND FEEL THAT YOU HAVE THE MOST PRECIOUS THING NEXT TO YOU: YOUR SMARTPHONE!

BOTTOM LINE: IF DINOSAURS HAVE CELL PHONES, THEY WON'T BE INTERESTED IN GLACIATION!

EVE, YOUR WICKEDNESS IS ALMOST LIKE MINE... I ADMIRE YOUR HATRED!

PREHISTORIC BULLIES IN ITS ENTIRETY.

WE SHOULD ORDER A LOT OF THEM AND GIVE THEM AS GIFTS... AND THEN WE WILL SEND THEM ALL NOTIFICATIONS TO KEEP THEM UNDER CONTROL.

AND INFORM THEM THAT THE ICE AGE IS JUST THE INVENTION OF A STUPID KID FROM NEW YORK!

I WILL GO BACK TO THE BUS STOP AND TRY TO GO BACK TO THE FUTURE! WITH MY PARENTS' CREDIT CARD, I WILL ORDER CELL PHONES ON AMAZON AND ASK FOR DELIVERY BY DRONE!

I LOVE DIABOLICAL PLANS. THE PREHISTORIC WORLD WILL EVOLVE FOR THE WORSE. THEY WILL FACE A NEW DICTATORSHIP: THE TECNOLOGICAL ONE! AND WE WILL BE ITS LEADERS!

JURASSIK DIARIES

"We will use underground tunnels, bringing inside enough food and timber to heat the corridors and then we will set up a central room with a huge fire that will always be fed. We will do this until the glaciation is over."

I hope I made myself clear.

Rapto touches his teeth that never stop hurting and asks me: "Martin, when the cold comes, can I make snowmen out of sand?" The usual joker!

I'm laughing out loud, Rapto is a born comedian and he can be funny even during difficult moments.

I resume my lesson and explain: "To be able to save ourselves, everyone will have to do their part. We will have to help each other and stop saying that nature made us hunters. It's time to grow up and be part of the same family!"
Waldo, Trisha, and Rapto applaud me, but the others get up and leave the classroom.

Nooooo!

"Where are you going?" I ask. "To get the cell phones!" answers Spin, the brontosaurus who dreams of opening the first pizzeria of prehistoric times.

CRS
PIZZA
DONUTS
TACOS
BP
BRONTO PIZZA
Bronto Pizza
Bronto Pizza
I'll offer you a great pizza... Do you have money? Can someone hurry up and invent money?
Bronto Pizza

JURASSIK DIARIES

I leave the classroom and sadly I see the drone drop off a big box with all kinds of smartphones inside.
The dinosaurs crowd to get their cell phones.
"Games! So many games!
There are so many!" says Bronto happily. The other dinosaurs are also happy and don't want to hear my sad stories about the glaciation.
Now they have their toys.

EVERYONE IS HAPPY!

NOBODY WANTS TO THINK ABOUT GLACIATION.

"Without a doubt, the greatest invention in the history of mankind is the cell phone. Oh, surely the wheel was also a great invention, but the wheel is not as good as the cell phone!" says Fester, the stegosaurus who once dreamed of building the first prehistoric car.
I'm disappointed, they all seem to be out of their minds.
I won't be able to stop the glaciation if everyone is distracted by cell phones.
I need an idea, but before I have time to think of one, more horrible news arrives.

BAD NEWS COMING!

HERE WE GO AGAIN! NO TIME TO RELAX!

CHAPTER FIVE

"The smartphones have memes made by Mr. No!" says Spike joyfully, the prehistoric computer engineer who, after the revelation of fire, discovered hot water.

IF THEY ASK AROUND:
SPIKE INVENTED HOT WATER. A TRUE GENIUS!

"Memes?" I ask.
"Yes, they have super fun memes from Mr. No!"
"About what?"
"Obviously about the glaciation!"
"He wants to influence all the dinosaurs!"
"In the fastest way!"
"And also the quickest!"
Are you ready to see them? With these no one, I mean no one, will take the extinction of the species seriously and it will be a disaster.

If you have nothing else to do, browse through the next 4 pages and discover the memes of the diabolical Mr. No!

JURASSIK DIARIES

MEME N.1

When you want to divert attention away from a problem and say the most stupid thing.

CHAPTER FIVE

MEME N.2

When you want to divert attention away from a problem and say **MORE** of the most stupid things.

JURASSIK DIARIES

MEME N.3

When you would do anything to deny the existence of glaciation.

> I ALREADY SHUDDER AT THE THOUGHT OF TOMORROW BEING THIS HOT AGAIN!

CHAPTER FIVE

MEME N.4

When you start to draw attention away from the same problem as before, but you are almost ridiculous.

JURASSIK DIARIES

This is absurd! No one is going to follow me and everyone is going to find Mr. No funny. His memes are really convincing in a dishonest way.

There aren't enough natural tunnels to save all of the prehistoric animals, and to build new ones, I'll have to invent excavators.

It won't be possible to stop the glaciation if only Waldo, Rapto, Lloyd, and Trisha are willing to follow me.

I know that there is a solution for everything and I start thinking.

I AM THINKING... BUT I CAN'T CONCENTRATE...

Who knows if in the modern world the new FIFA for PS has been released! What is wrong with my brain?!

I have to concentrate on serious things and come up with a plan that will allow me to convince everyone that the ice age is real and imminent. Soon the world will be a huge ice cream cone and everyone is laughing in front of cell phones.

"Of course!" I rejoice, as if I had won the Super Bowl. The solution, as always, is simple, you just have to figure it out. I call my friends in front of the blackboard and explain my brilliant plan to them.

"Guys, I know that Mr. No's memes are convincing and hilarious... and I know that he has become the most followed influencer of

CHAPTER FIVE

prehistory. This is possible because he has Ade, Eve, and Mike at his disposal. They are the technology experts and they are the ones who made him popular. If I had been Phil the nerd, a dear friend of mine, I would have hacked into their cell phones and posted some memes about glaciation. I would have explained the reality, but I am not a hacker and in order to access Mr. No's account and post memes with the truth, I would have to steal his phone.
There is no other solution."

Rapto trembles at the idea and asks me: "Do you want to go back to the village of the darkists and risk being devoured? How will you get back into their city?"

"That place is full of bullies and carnivorous animals!" adds Waldo. "Maybe we should invent a plane and fly to another planet. I can already see the four of us on the Moon playing Magic. That would be great."

PLAYING CARDS ON THE MOON? COOL!!!

Trisha gets angry, grinds her teeth and, with her usual determination, says: "This is our world and we are not running anywhere. We will save the planet from the glaciation and steal the cell phone from that tyrant of a T-Rex!"

WE WILL FIGHT BEFORE WE GIVE UP... WE WILL FIGHT. AND WITH HIS CELL PHONE WE WILL CONVINCE EVERYONE.

"But...how can we do that?" asks Rapto shakily, still worn out by the kidnapping. I intervene and stand in front of the blackboard. "This time we will make them come to us and they will deliver the cell phone into our hands."
"What do you have in mind?" Trisha asks me.
What I have in mind is a highly intelligent plan, so much so that I can't even believe how well my brain works.

CHAPTER FIVE

"We will give Mr. No and the bullies new cell phones in exchange for the old ones. We will tell them that the new ones have super special functions and then we will steal Mike's smartphone data. Then we will communicate with everyone from Mr. No's profile!"

THE SOLUTION TO OUR PROBLEMS IS CALLED *INNOVATION!* WHEN PEOPLE BUY A CELL PHONE, THE NEXT A DAY MUCH NICER ONE COMES OUT THAT COSTS HALF AS MUCH... AND EVERYBODY WANTS THAT ONE! THAT'S HOW WE WILL BRING THEM TO US!

Does this cell phone run out of battery too often? BUY A NEW ONE!

The world will then be populated by a generation of idiots!

JURASSIK DIARIES

Trisha is puzzled and explains her doubts: "They will know that it's us... they will recognize us."

"Let me explain the second part of the plan and you will understand why they won't recognize us. We will say that we just arrived from the future on the 'magic' bus and we will be wearing disguises. Really great disguises."

MY DISGUISE

THE HAIR LOOKS MORE LIKE A *MAD* SCIENTIST THAN A *COMPUTER* SCIENTIST.

SO FROM NOW ON I WILL BE CARL THE COMPUTER SCIENTIST!

IF PEOPLE DON'T KNOW *CLARK KENT* IS *SUPERMAN* WITH GLASSES ON, WHY WOULD I BE RECOGNIZED BY DUMB BULLIES?

COMPUTER LAB COAT

WHAT'S HE TRYING TO SAY HERE?

CHAPTER FIVE

Trisha has a good laugh and Rapto seems almost jealous because she didn't laugh as much at his jokes.
But I am not joking and I point out: "There is nothing to laugh about. My plan is perfect. As Carl the computer scientist, I will set up a booth at the entrance of Jurassika and, when they arrive, I will try to sell them the new cell phones that I have built, but I will ask for the old ones in exchange. I won't sell them the new ones unless they give me the old ones."
"Brilliant!" says Waldo, "You are a brilliant boy. One day I will take you flying around Jurassika. You deserve it!"

I look at my friend and smile: "Waldo, you don't fly! Remember that. You don't want to find yourself in a ravine!"
Trisha is always the liveliest and most interested in every detail, and she asks me: "So we will also have disguises?"
Waldo lights up and talks over her: "Yes!!! I love disguises! I also want one!"
"Sure!" I clarify to everybody, "You Trisha will become Sally, the marketing manager of my company."
"What?"
"You will simply list a series of numbers and say words like 'growth' and 'decrease' once in a while. You will have to make them understand how the new cell phone will change the lives of those who buy it."
"How will I be dressed?"

PROFESSIONAL TRICERATOPS BRIEFCASE!
YOU, TRISHA, WILL BECOME SALLY, THE MARKETING MANAGER OF MY COMPANY!
What if I pretend to be the president of the prehistoric world?

CHAPTER FIVE

"You will be dressed elegantly. Everyone will stop to look at you. You'll have to make them believe that the numbers show that you can't be successful and happy without our new cell phone."
"Can I speak with a French accent? I've always liked it!"
"Of course! It will help hide your identity!"
"Can I say that I have a driver?"
"We haven't invented the car yet!"
"Ah, true... I forgot that you abandoned the project! But it fit a marketing manager!"
I turn to Waldo.
I look at him and he blushes with shame, he's exuberant, but shy at the same time.
"Who am I going to be?" he asks me.
I pause... and the wait almost makes my friend faint.
"You will be the key to my perfect plan!"
"Tell me...tell me, I'm curious!"
"You will be..."
"I will be?"
"You will be the client who wants to buy the cell phone at all costs!"
"What?"
Waldo doesn't understand and I try to explain myself better.
"You're going to play a customer and get Mr. No interested in our new cell phone. You're going to want the smartphone at all costs."

JURASSIK DIARIES

"How will I dress?"
"In an unrecognizable way!"

> You could have told me that I would be a woman!

Waldo is happy. "I told you I love disguises. Can I enrich my character with details?"
"Like?"
"Like all actors, I'm going to get into the character and I'm going to need the details of her life. Maybe my name is Sophia and I have a boyfriend, a very boring pterodactyl, who left me because

CHAPTER FIVE

we didn't talk much, since they are incomprehensible. Perhaps I can also add a British accent... because I come from a family of noble brontosaurus."
Waldo is really exuberant, creative, and I nod.

WALDO WILL DISGUISE HIMSELF AS A VERY, VERY RICH BRITISH BRONTOSAURUS!

I am sure he will be perfect in the role of "Sophia, the customer!" Rapto touches his teeth, and I know that his mouth bandage could be a problem for the disguise.
My friend approaches me and asks: "Will I be playing a comedian?"
"Rapto, you will be the technician and my assistant. You will also have a lab coat and a helmet, so they won't see your headband."
Rapto is happy to be close to me... and who wouldn't be!

I MIGHT BE EXAGGERATING A LITTLE.
THIS CELL PHONE HAS 27 INTEGRATED CAMERAS AND 2 MILLION GIGABYTES OF MEMORY.

CHAPTER FIVE

Rapto jumps with joy and asks me: "Should I exaggerate the cell phone's performance abilities?"
"You can exaggerate... you have to be a liar, of course, to retrieve Mr. No's cell phone!"
"I wouldn't call myself a liar. I would prefer to call myself someone who lives on the other side of the facts."
I laugh!
Waldo always manages to find the right, funny words.

MARK TWAIN, A BETTER HUMORIST THAN PHILIP OSBOURNE, WROTE: "IF YOU ALWAYS TELL THE TRUTH, YOU DON'T HAVE TO REMEMBER ANYTHING!" BUT RAPTO CAN MAKE AN EXCEPTION AND TELL LIES TO SAVE THE PLANET.

Now the plan is organized and the roles are clear, we just have to build a fake booth at the entrance of Jurassika and put a sign next to it saying: "On sale tomorrow, the newest and most powerful cell phone in the world."

JURASSIK DIARIES

I hug my friends, walk out of the classroom, watch the sunset, and sit on the floor thinking.
Trisha approaches and sits next to me, she gives me a smile and a tender look.
Then she asks me: "Are you worried about something? Your plan seems perfect to me!"
Usually, my plans are perfect, but I make mistakes, too...
I look at her and with a sly smile I answer her: "I've forgotten that we need a cell phone that looks super cool!"
Trisha comforts me with the right words: "Every great idea has a great flaw. But yours is so big that it makes the project ridiculous. But don't worry, we'll find a solution!"
She has a strange way of consoling me...
"I got it!" I scream.
I get up and start dancing as if I were in a disco.
"What's the matter with you?"
"I have a cell phone...we simply have to modify it and I know how to do it!"

MIKE AND THE T-REX DANCE
MIKE DOESN'T DANCE LIKE I DO...

CHAPTER FIVE

I'M NOT TRYING TO DANCE BETTER THAN ANYONE ELSE. I TRY TO DANCE BETTER THAN I DO MYSELF!

THIS IS THE T-REX DANCE AND YOU'RE LUCKY YOU DON'T HEAR THE BACKGROUND MUSIC!

ARE YOU READY FOR THE
IS THE WO
FOR JURAS

"I am the only one missing!"

P.S. HOWEVER, WHEN YOU THINK ABOUT IT, THEY COULD HAVE PUT A MASK ON SUPERMAN

RDS OF DISGUISE?

O READY

K BOYS?

YES

NO

AND YOU, ARE YOU READY? CROSS OUT YOUR ANSWER

EFFECTIVELY...

JURASSIK DIARIES

We are clever and intelligent and we manage to organize the presentation event for our new cell phone that we call "iPooh," as a tribute to Winnie the Pooh.
As we imagined, all the T-Rexes came out of the village and lined up in front of the booth.
Mr. No and the bullies are the first to arrive.
Eve is the most curious and says: "I really want to see this great phone! On the poster it says that it can photograph a page of a book a thousand yards away, even at night."

Ade laughs and says: "What do you need it for? You don't read books, even during the day and two feet away."
Mr. No arrives at the booth and looks at me. He won't recognize me with my Clark Kent glasses, or else we will have to accept the people who write Superman have been making fun of us the whole time.
"Hey, brat, get your new cell phone out!" Mr. No says to me.
In a scholarly manner, I say to him: "Please, call me Carl! My assistant Took or Elisa, our marketing manager, will explain the benefits you will get with our new smartphone."
Trisha, with a tag hanging on her coat with the name Elisa written on it, smiles at the three bullies and Mr. No and says:

CHAPTER FIVE

"I'll be brief. You now recharge your cell phones with batteries that sooner or later will run out, because electricity has not yet been invented, but the iPooh is rechargeable with solar energy! Just leave it under the sun and it will charge!"

"WOOOWWWW!!" all the T-Rexes say in unison. They are amazed!

It's so hot!*

Let's say that leaving it under the sun can have its disadvantages... But we don't tell the darkists!

BOOM!

* If the sun also says so...

JURASSIK DIARIES

Waldo arrives, who plays the part of Sophia the customer, and starts shouting in the crowd: "Get out of my way! I want to buy it first. I'm so rich, so rich that if I were to give birth, I would make a golden egg!"
Mr. No glowers at Waldo, and immediately threatens him: "I'm a darkist...did you hear that? You may be a nice brontosaurus, but we got here first and we're stronger. If you don't feel like becoming a meat skewer, turn around and go back to your city!" Waldo smiles and says: "Thank you for the compliments, but I must have it first."
So I step in according to the plan and explain: "The one who will give me a hundred dry branches, fifteen coconuts, and exchange their old cell phone will have it."
Mike takes his smartphone, the one with Mr. No's Instagram account, puts it on the counter and calls the darkists who bring a cart with everything I asked for.
Too bad that the cart does not have round but rectangular wheels, it is clear that they still don't understand the difference between a circle and a square. I am speechless!
Rapto, who plays my assistant, with a helmet on his head that allows him not to be recognized, takes Mike's cell phone with incredible speed and hides it under the counter, where a pterodactyl puts it in his mouth and, after a few seconds, takes off to bring it to a shelter. Yeah! Plan accomplished!
We give them the new cell phone, which doesn't work, and quickly

CHAPTER FIVE

sneak away while the darkists surround Mr. No to admire the iPooh. The T-Rexes gawked at the phone, but somehow could not understand that the glaciation was coming.
The new iPooh won't be able to do the thinking for them either.

> FINALLY I HAVE THE NEW IPOOH! NOW I CAN NAVIGATE SUPER-FAST AND DRAW WITH MY NAILS. I CAN EVEN MEASURE THE DISTANCE BETWEEN THE EARTH AND THE MOON AND SEE THE WEATHER!

> You don't want to see the weather...You've got a nice global glaciation on the way... and you'd be a denier. I bet...!

JURASSIK DIARIES

We take shelter in Jurassika, enter the classroom, and we all look for the password to access Mike's phone, then we will get into Mr. No's profile and tell all the dinosaurs that the glaciation is real and everyone will have to give us a helping hand to dig the tunnels.

HOW CAN WE SAVE THE WORLD IF WE ARE NOT ALL UNITED? YOU SHOULD START TO OPEN OUR EYES!

Waldo suggests: "Maybe the password is 'Noglaciation!'"
I try it: it's wrong!
Nothing we can do.
"Maybe," suggests Trisha, "it's 'Schoolsucks.'"
I'll try this password too... nothing.
Rapto approaches, touches his teeth and then says:
"What if he is so trivial that he has chosen 'Password'?"
We have a laugh, who is stupid enough to use the word 'password' as the password?
I type it and... yes, we found it!
I congratulate our comedian and I say to him: "You're right, Rapto! Mike could never have remembered any other word but 'password.'
Very well! Now it's time to post our memes about glaciation, obviously retouching Mr. No's pictures!"

CHAPTER FIVE

MEME N. 1 (THE AWARENESS)

**Fight the GLACIATION!
Come build the SAFETY TUNNELS!**

> IT'S SO COLD THAT I WENT OUT WITH THE DOG AND CAME BACK WITH A PENGUIN!

JURASSIK DIARIES

MEME N. 2 (THE AWARENESS)

Fight the **GLACIATION!**
Come build the **SAFETY TUNNELS!**

CHAPTER FIVE

MEME N. 3 (THE AWARENESS)

Fight the GLACIATION!
Come build the SAFETY TUNNELS!

JURASSIK DIARIES

3RD AUGUST

All the dinosaurs gather in front of the school and are ready to help us save the planet from the ice age. They are all smiling and have signs that say: "The glaciation is real!" and "Don't freeze in front of the glaciation."
The memes were more effective than any lesson or speech I could give.
I don't know if it's right or wrong, but I'm happy because now everybody is working toward the same goal.

WILL T-REXES EVER UNDERSTAND THAT NO APP CAN HELP THEM BECOME FREE AND LEARN TO LOVE?

A smartphone turns out to be more useful than any of the arguments I've started, which should have taught me to keep it hidden instead of just waving it around in my hand, because just then a darkist pterodactyl grabs it and takes off into the sky. How unexpected!
Without the smartphone, we will be back in the hands of Mr. No! His account, even if it seems crazy, affects the whole planet. "No!" I scream, "Mr. No sent a darkist to sneak in and take his cell phone back. We must get it back before he returns it."

CHAPTER FIVE

None of the dinosaurs want to fight against Mr. No.
They are scared of their leader and of the bullies. So how do I stop the pterodactyl?
He is heading into the enchanted valley and after that it will be impossible for me to understand where he is going.
"I'm going after him!" says Waldo fearlessly.
Everyone is laughing at him.
It's not fair to make fun of him just because he's not a bird.

Waldo pulls out his pair of paper wings and continues:
"I'll bring the smartphone home."
Nobody believes his words.
He is a brontosaurus but Waldo is convinced he can do it and, like the hero of a movie, he concludes: "Only those who have no imagination do not have wings to fly."
Waldo flies in the sky like the most graceful of birds.
Okay, maybe I'm exaggerating.
Let's say that paper wings allow Waldo to soar through the air.

I feel like a seagull, looking down on you from above, little humans and dinosaurs, who believe they are demigods... but you can't even fly!
?

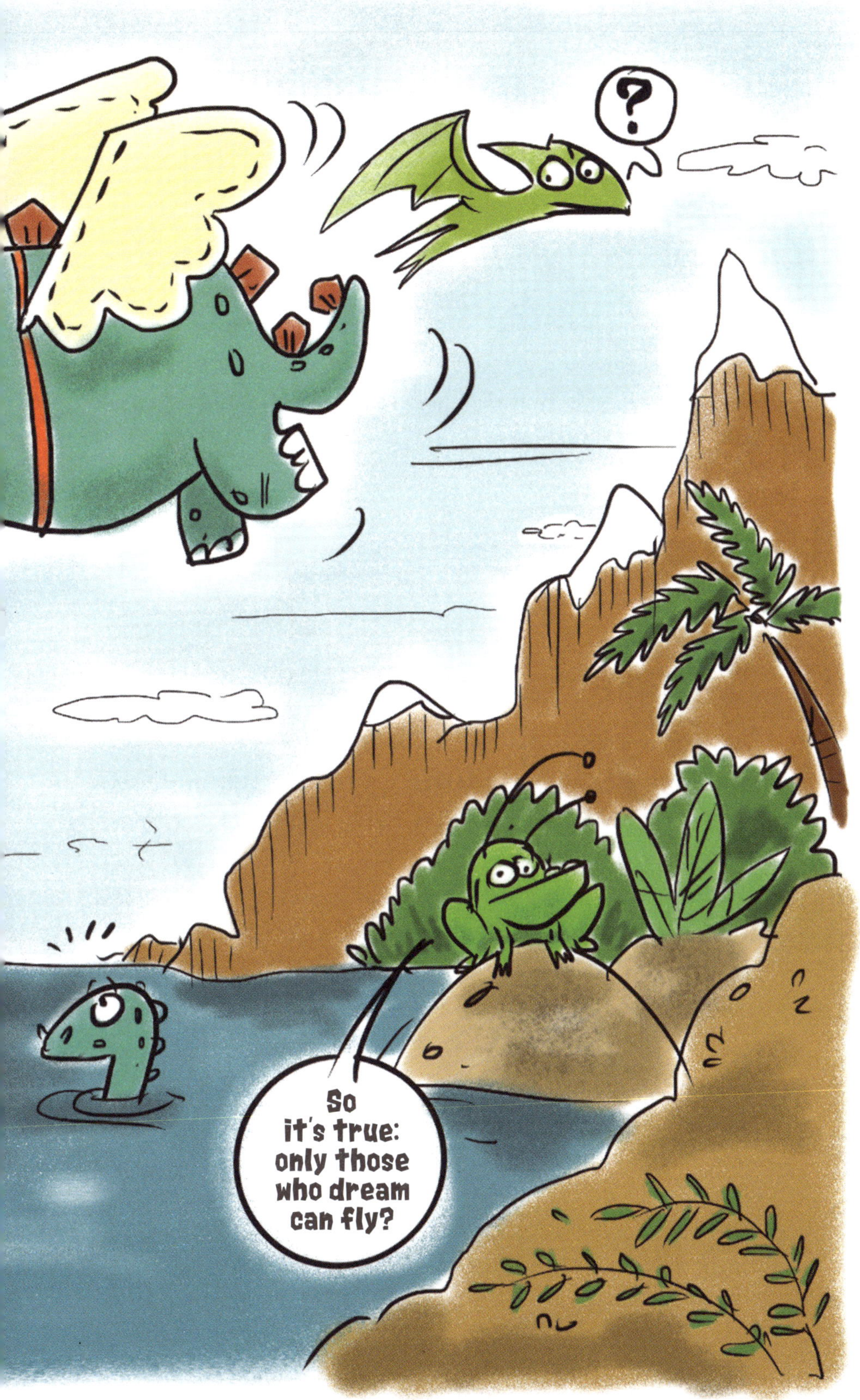
?
So it's true: only those who dream can fly?

JURASSIK DIARIES

My little friend lets everyone know his happiness and repeats: "Flying is awesome! Flying is awesome... and for those who still have doubts... flying is awesome!"
One of the dinosaurs present at the gathering, perhaps a little more practical, yells to him: "Think about getting the cell phone back!"

WALDO LOVES TO FLY AND TO HELP HIS FRIENDS. HE DOESN'T LACK COURAGE... HE LACKS ONLY WINGS!

The darkist pterodactyl does not worry about Waldo's arrival, on the contrary, he enjoys it because my friend's flight is clumsy. Ptero mocks him by rotating close to him and moving away when my friend tries to grab him.
My cute brontosaurus is not someone who gives up easily and does not care at all for the pterodactyl's attitude.
Waldo inhales, takes in all the air he can, closes his eyes and suddenly turns over, crashing into the darkist.
Wow! It looks like an arrow that hits a bullseye.
Both of them fall quickly towards the lake of piranhas below them.
"Nooooo!" screams Waldo.

ONLY RODACTYLS CAN FLY!
H...H... How do you fly in the water?
YOU DON'T FLY, MY DEAR!

JURASSIK DIARIES

The razor-like teeth of the piranhas flash before their eyes. They know that those horrible creatures bite with great strength and tear even the strongest armor to pieces, because they are Jurassic piranhas.
They are not small, and look like sharks, but nastier.
The sound of Waldo and Ptero hitting the water is loud and water splashes Trisha, Rapto, and myself in the face, even though we are watching from the top of a cliff.
"What now?" Rapto asks me concerned. "What will become of Waldo?"
"I'll get him out and bring him home!" I say to everyone, hoping to reassure them.

Trisha, who is always skeptical, asks me: "How?"
"With science. If not, what else?" I answer.
I pull a diving mask with a snorkel out of my backpack and say: "With this! Before I ended up here, in Jurassika, I was on my way to my grandma's. We were planning on going to see the ocean."

FROM NOW ON, NO MORE HEAD IN THE CLOUDS!

ARMORED ANTI-PIRANHA T-SHIRT

NOTE TO THE READER: IF YOU'RE THINKING OF GOING DIVING LIKE MARTIN, REMEMBER THAT ANYONE WHO WANTS IT WILL GO UNDERWATER, BUT ONLY THOSE WHO CAN SWIM WILL COME BACK UP! SO, HAVE AN ADULT ACCOMPANY YOU IF YOU WANT TO DIVE, OR STAY HOME AND READ A NICE BOOK BY *PHILIP OSBOURNE*.

CHAPTER FIVE

I'm afraid to dive off the cliff, but Waldo doesn't come out of the water. He might not be able to swim, or maybe he was already eaten by piranhas. "Come on, jump!" Trisha says to me.
She makes it sound easy, but my legs are trembling. 
Why do I have to be the hero?
I try to understand how many meters of height there are between me and the sea. Just then a nice T-Rex came by to encourage me, but he bumps my chest and I lose my balance and fall.
"Heeeeelp!" 
Trisha is laughing her head off. I see her amused, and I shout to her: "What are you laughing about?"
"You know how to breathe in water, but do you know how not to be devoured by piranhas?"
Great question and, dear diary, even if I have the answer, I will tell you in a few minutes.

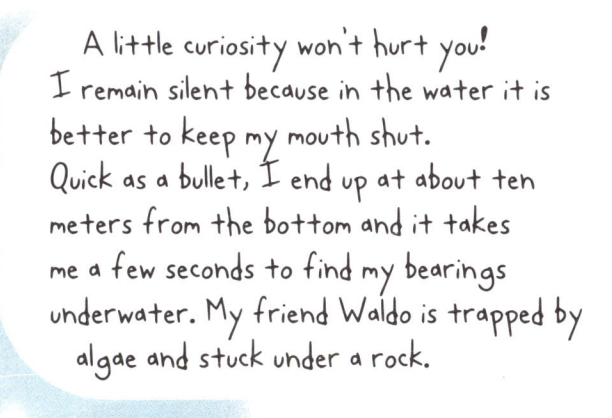

A little curiosity won't hurt you!
I remain silent because in the water it is better to keep my mouth shut.
Quick as a bullet, I end up at about ten meters from the bottom and it takes me a few seconds to find my bearings underwater. My friend Waldo is trapped by algae and stuck under a rock.

Oops...I just wanted to know the time...

IT'S TWO O'CLOCK!

JURASSIK DIARIES

Luckily, he is less than one meter from the surface.
He isn't breathing, so with all my strength, I swim over to him, wishing I had taken swimming lessons at some point.
I breathe through the snorkel, and I try to push him up, because I want to get his nostrils above the water.
Exhausted, I manage to make him re-emerge.
He breathes and suddenly wakes up.
"Where am I?" he asks me.
"You are safe!" I reassure him, as a true hero would do.
I am happy!

I save my friend and Mike's phone before the water destroys it. I change the password of Mr. No's account and then quickly delete it!

WHY DON'T THEY GIVE US AN *OSCAR* IN REAL LIFE WHEN WE DO GOOD DEEDS?

Martin

CHAPTER FIVE

No one will be able to use his profile anymore.
Mission accomplished!

Now it's time to go back to my prehistoric friends and build the tunnels that will save us from the ice age.
Nothing and no one can stop us.
At least I think so...until the snow begins to fall.
Suddenly fear fills my friends' eyes, and I invite them all to hide in the natural tunnels.
We did not have time to bring in the supplies or to build enough tunnels for everyone.
I will come up with a plan B after we get as many animals as possible sheltered.
My crew and I manage to get a hundred T-Rexes, brontosaurus, etc. into the natural tunnels.
We are cool!
It doesn't look like it will ever stop snowing, but after only three hours, the sun came back out and started warming things up again.
How is this possible?
The glaciation has not arrived! ROAR!
It was a false alarm.
Am I sure that the Jurassic world became extinct with the glaciation?

JURASSIK DIARIES

I see small meteorites falling on the ground. I get closer and I realize that I was wrong.
No! I can't be wrong!

COMING!!!

SMALL BUT TOUGH METEORITES!

I really don't like this!
What if the dinosaurs had become extinct because of meteorites?
Maybe the school books were always wrong!
Scientists can be wrong sometimes.
I have to think of a new plan and implement it before the Earth becomes a parking lot for space stones.
I already have a thousand IDEAS TO SAVE THE WORLD in my head and all of them are flawless, because, of course, I am Martin and I always have the right solution to save the world.

NOTE TO MYSELF: REMEMBER NOT TO LISTEN TO THE DARKISTS AND THEN INVENT SOCCER!

Meanwhile, I take advantage of this and teach everyone how to throw snowballs. We have fun throwing them at each other. The T-Rexes, with their short arms, are not good at this game.
They will have to learn how to lose!

Get ready for this bomb, Mr. No!
My God... How SCARY!
MIKE, HERE I AM!
3...2...1 EVE, SAY GOODBYE TO THIS WORLD! HA HA HA!
PHEW... I CAN'T THROW IT FAR!
...and they all played happily ever after (with snowballs)

JURASSIK DIARIES

The bullies show up again.
Ade, Eve, and Mike always show up when there is a game to play, never when they have to study.
We are happy and when we finish rolling around in the snow, I call Waldo, Rapto, Trisha, and the others. I want them to follow me to the classroom where I will explain my new project:
"Subjugate the meteorites!"
I can't even start with: "I'll save you from the meteorites!" before the darkists are yelling at me: "There are no meteorites!"
They haven't changed and are more aggressive than ever. They don't believe in anything!
It's time for a new plan!

NOTE TO MYSELF:

REMEMBER TO DEFEAT THE DARKISTS AND DON'T STOP BELIEVING IN DREAMS, AFTER ALL, IT ONLY TAKES ONE STEP TO REACH THE STARS... AND TO DESTROY THE METEORITES!

CHAPTER FIVE

The new lessons!

SUBJUGATE THE METEORITES!

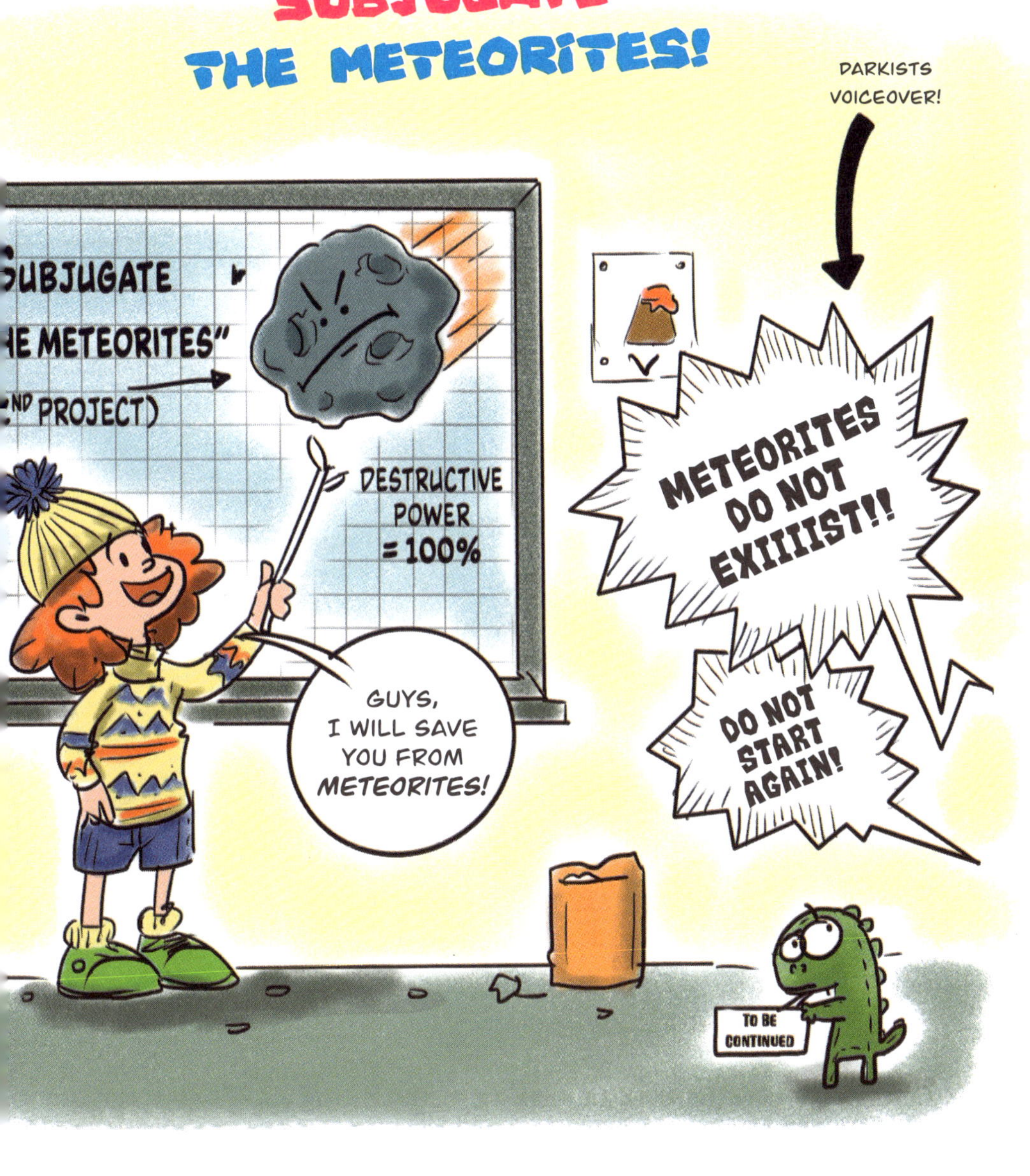

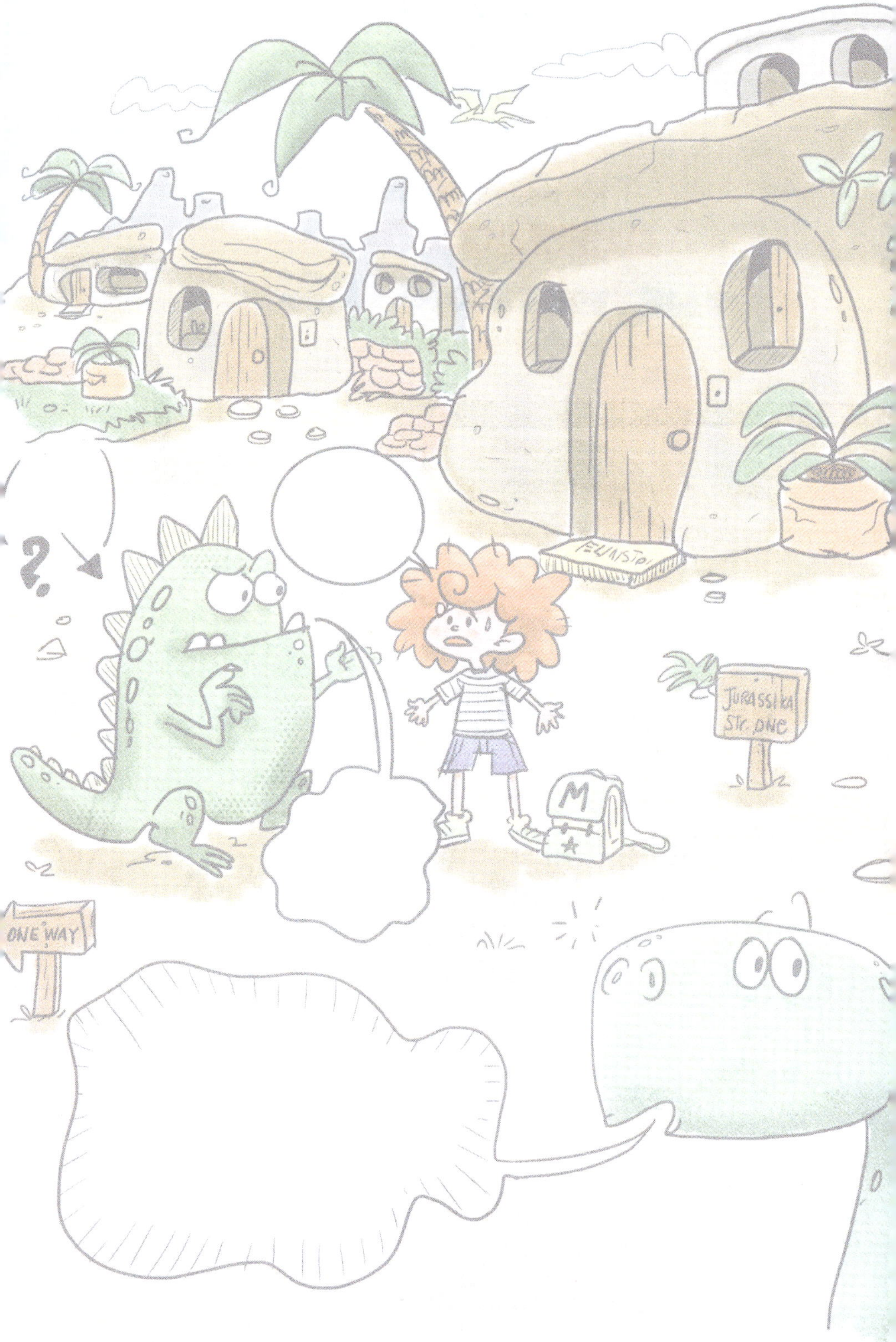
JURASSIKA
STR. ONE
ONE WAY

PHILIP OSBOURNE

JURASSIK DIARIES

Illustrations by Roberta Procacci

A NEW WORLD

PHILIP OSBOURNE THE WRITER

Philip Osbourne is a worldwide best-selling author.
For many years, he has been working on movie screenplays and comic books for the American market, among others "Jenna" with Jim Fern and Joe Rubinstein featuring the original score by Iron Maiden's Paul Di Anno, as well as articles for cinema magazines ("Empire") and pitches for movie projects together with film guru Brian Yuzna. Osbourne's books are published in over 45 countries, including USA, France, Italy, Germany, Greece, Russia, Romania, Brazil, China, Albania and is now the author of the official books "Harry & Bunnie" and "ABC Monster", two cartoons produced by Animasia.
His best-selling book series "Diary of a Nerd" will soon be a TV series (produced by Rainbow) for the international markets. "Jurassik Diaries" will be a cartoon.
The success of Philip Osbourne's book adaptations strongly continues in TV and Movies.

ROBERTA PROCACCI THE ARTIST

Roberta Procacci is an illustrator of children's books.
She became known thanks to the drawings and comics present in "Diary of a Nerd", a work published in 39 countries. Over the years, she has illustrated guides for children and even amusing books on science ("Small family experiments" by Francesco Laurenzi, published by Gremese Editore). A very prolific illustrator, Roberta Procacci recently published "Alice & Cuore" by Martin Steel (Edizioni Zona Franca).
She has already collaborated with Philip Osbourne on "Ghosts & Bulli" (Peruzzo Editor) and "The Lord of the Night and the Bullies" (Armando Curcio editor).
The latter, an illustrated novel, based on a true story, was considered by critics to be of great value.

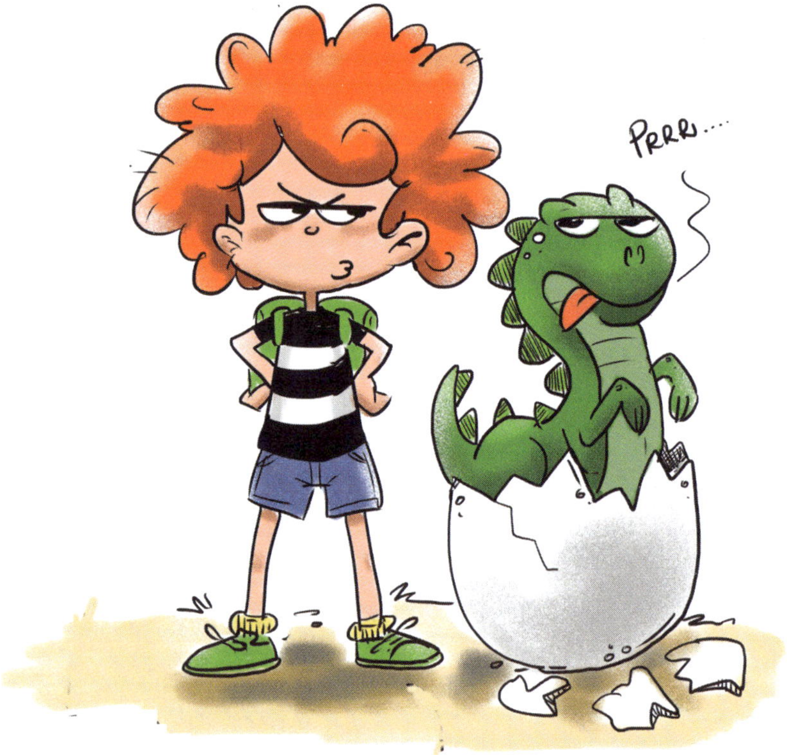
PRRR....